Warrior Alien Passion

I0543790

By Sharon Barrington

Shelbi MacPhadden Adventure 4

Published by:
ESIL Publishing,
638 Buchan Avenue, Oshawa, Ontario L1J 3A3

The characters and situations portrayed in this book are fictional. Any resemblance to persons living or dead is purely coincidental.

This book contains an excerpt from the forthcoming book *Rebel Alien Passion* by Sharon

Barrington. This except has been developed for this edition only and may not reflect the final version in the forthcoming book.

Barrington, Sharon

Ebook ISBN: 978-0-9683356-7-3
Softcover ISBN: 5972-1-999550-8-3

Table of Contents

Dear Reader,

Thank you for downloading my book, WARRIOR ALIEN, PASSION.

As you read it, I hope you have a sensual moment, perhaps a grin, or some warm personal feeling as you join Shelbi MacPhadden in her next adventure in a new alien world of intrigue, passionate, and love making.

Sit down, lie back or enjoy reading it where ever you feel comfortable to be stimulated for the sheer joy of sweet physical passionate sex.

If this story brought a smile to your lips, or a thrill to any part of your body or just a moment of sexual fantasy, then I have made a small difference in your life. To me that is a great feeling and why I write these stories.

To enjoy yourself some more, get the next alien erotica romance adventure of Shelbi MacPhadden, look for it on Amazon Kindle soon.

Here is to your personal excitement and passion!

Sharon Barrington

Chapter 1 War and Soapy Sex

The silver bullets ricocheted dangerously close to her right leg. She threw herself down to the red earth. The pain radiating from slamming her breasts rolled across her chest. She could not fail! Shelbi had come too far to lose it all now.

The two soldiers that had followed her into this potential death trap also lay prone on the hard earth. She was their leader and they would follow her, even if it meant their premature death. Soon, three of her squad would die. That was part of her plan and necessary if she was going to win the war.

Shelbi and her companions shimmied along the dry dirt floor of the battle field, thankful they had covered the metallic parts of their war uniforms so no reflection would be a target for dreaded enemy snipers.

At the planned moment, Shelbi broke radio silence and barked one word, "Butterfly!"

Seconds later, three of her squad had jumped up, arms spread like butterflies with their gun laser beams ricocheting out across the landscape. Now they lay dead on the hard earth, mortally wounded by the enemy's return fire.

Before the firing subsided, Shelbi and her two companions slipped up on the enemy squad, pinning them down with their rifles. Then bang, bang, bang. Three bullets. Three dead enemy soldiers.

Each of Shelbi's remaining squad reached out and took a blue armband off the dead soldiers. They slipped them over their green armbands.

Now for the second stage of Shelbi's strategic battle attack plan.

They walked into the enemy's camp near the medical tent. As Shelbi had anticipated, a waiting ambulance sat with its motor running, but with no one inside. Shelbi opened the door and jumped into the driver's seat. One team soldier jumped into the passenger side and one leapt into the empty stretcher in the back.

Moving out quickly, Shelbi drove the ambulance soundlessly through the war zone. As they rounded the corner on the road to the major's tent, Shelbi flipped the switch on the ambulance's flashing red lights.

As she had planned and hoped, when they drove up to the guards posted at the gate, they automatically opened it and the ambulance was waved through. No identification necessary.

They pulled up to the major's command centre, parked the ambulance, and left it running. They moved inside quickly with their rifles at parade rest. As they entered the major's building, they took off the blue armbands leaving the green ones exposed.

Shelbi expected no one would notice. They moved quickly down the grey corridors and into the major's command centre. Again, three helmeted warriors walked forward and no one challenged them. Moments later, Shelbi was elbow to elbow with the major with her gun pointed at him. Her two companions were tight behind, using their arms to lock themselves together, as they pressed against her back.

Shelbi spoke softly, "Major, surrender or die!"

The major spoke one word, "Brittle!"

Guns blazed and Shelbi's two companions were frozen on the spot. The umpire drone pronounced them dead.

Shelbi looked at the major again and affirmed, "I won't ask you again, Major. Surrender or die!"

The major looked at the two dead companions leaning against Shelbi and realized, *"My stars, the game is over! We will never get a shot at her without her taking me out. Nothing left but to gracefully surrender."*

He laughed heartily. His left hand reached down and flipped the protective cover off the red surrender scanner patch. His left handprint on the glass patch was recognized. The umpire drones noted the strategic action he was taking and his unconditional surrender.

The War Games Umpire system immediately locked down all rifles and guns in the war zone. All the warriors who had been frozen and pronounced dead had their battle suits unfrozen and were free to move.

The major turned and looked at Shelbi. With a slight smile on his weathered face, he said, "Private Shelbi, it would be my honour to have lunch with you tomorrow and discover just what's going on in that head of yours. After 12 cycles, 12 wars, I've never even been close to surrendering. You managed to capture me with only three privates!"

Shelbi took off her helmet and looked at the major.

"Sir, it would be my privilege to have lunch with you. I may or may not divulge my strategy, but I can give you some ideas on how I came up with it."

Again, the major laughed. "Well done, Private Shelbi," he exclaimed to the room. Then he began to clap and the entire room clapped for the three privates that had taken down Major Michael Eric Sanderson, leader of the blue squad.

As Private Shelbi MacPhadden travelled back to the green squad command centre, she thought back to how she became part of the empire's warrior elite program.

The empire had specifically created the warrior princess group for women to be the military strategic elite but also relationship builders between Earth and new planets they uncovered as they expanded through the universe.

She'd liked growing up on Earth and playing with toys. As her body grew, she began to play more competitive games with girls and boys. Those games used computers and special military war games. She liked the action and feeling like she was part of the games.

By the time Shelbi was 13, her parents had a special space uniform moulded just for her. They had it adjusted as she grew through her teenage years. It fitted tightly to her body as it expanded to fit her broader hips and her growing breasts.

Then she began playing war games outdoors, not just computer simulations: roaming over the land, capturing the enemy, and taking their fort. Being a leader, shooting to kill.

Shelbi's first application for warrior princess was accepted gratefully by the tall athletic female empire warrior scout who had been tracking her progress. Most candidates were rejected on their first application. The Empire Warrior Princess Academy wanted to make sure their candidates really understood what they were applying for and not just following a fad.

Major Reneey Christina Weatherson, the empire warrior scout, had tracked Shelbi for a number of years. She was fully aware of Shelbi's hidden talents and she really wanted this military career. After a lengthy review of Major Reneey Weatherson's scout report and the unusual recommendation, the warrior princess's elite application committee had awarded Shelbi the honour of joining the empire's warrior princess elite program at the academy three months after her 19th birthday, just months after becoming eligible.

Shelbi arrived back at the barracks having been transported by the blue squad major's second in command. As the three victorious privates emerged from the armoured vehicle and began to walk into the building, the green squadron formed a line for her to walk down as they clapped and cheered. The green squad had never won a major battle against the blue squad. Now they won both the battle and the war.

Shelbi peeled off to walk towards her living quarters. As she walked down the grey green corridor, Brendenn, a bully she would like to decapitate, emerged from an adjoining corridor.

"Great job, Shelbi. You're lucky, squirt," Brendenn jested with a smirk on his handsome face.

Then, as usual, he reached down and grabbed her right ass cheek, lifting her up on her own toes. He laughed and walked quickly away with his three companions.

Shelbi was instantly fuming. She turned and yelled out, "Someday, Brendenn, you lizard, I will take you down hard!"

The very first time she saw Brendenn Corzann, he had turned around and grabbed her ass. He had done the same thing ever since. He was one year ahead of her and knew more about fighting and one-on-one combat than she did. She had signed up just recently for extra training on one-on-one combat and she was going to get him. A smile crossed her face when she thought of his pain as he lay face down on the hard corridor floor.

It'd been a long day of fighting and Shelbi was tired, but she knew she had to go to the victory dinner. As a squad leader, she had been promoted and had her own private room with its own shower. She stripped out of her field uniform and put it in the refresher. Then she walked naked into her shower and grabbed the green soap. *"I really need to feel the hot water soothing these tense muscles,"* she thought.

As she ran the soap over her tired arms, she began to fantasize about what she would do to Brendenn when she beat him. *"You will wish you never picked on Shelbi MacPhadden, you lizard,"* she thought with a smile creeping across her face.

As the hot water pummelled her breasts, she ran the soap over and around them, washing off the dirt, sweat, and grime. The more she lathered her grapefruit sized breasts, the more her red nipples began to tingle and harden. She began to imagine Brendenn taking the soap from her hands and gently caressing her soft breasts and sucking on her tense nipples. She began to flick her fingers over each pulsating nipple, imagining his tongue moving back and forth on each one sensually.

The tension began to rise as she thought of him standing in front of her naked. She could practically see the water running down his chiselled abs. She knew, at six foot five, he would tower over her and the very thought of his muscular body sent shivers down her spine. She decided to enjoy playing with herself.

She closed her eyes and began to imagine his fingers running down the inside of her thighs with the soap.

Then she began to think of taking charge. "Drop the soap, Brendenn," she imagined herself saying. Then she thought, *I'll turn him around and I'll slap his ass hard."*

She began to imagine soaping her soft breasts then running them up and down his warm slippery back, the solid muscles caressing her breasts and tickling her nipples. Shelbi imagined commanding him, "Put your arms to your side and leave them there now!" She could then reach around the front of his naked body and soap between his legs and around his hardening rod.

She could imagine the wonderful length and enormous thickness as she ran her soapy hands up and down his long shaft.

Her hand-to-hand combat was getting better and she knew one day she would surprise him and take him down, regardless of his three companions that always seemed to be with him.

As she towelled the water droplets off her body, she realized she hadn't satisfied herself. She would definitely have to take care of those feelings after the victory dinner. The wetness between her thighs told her that was a necessity. As she dried off her copper mound, the towel flicked against her erect bud.

She turned and flung herself on the bed. *"Why wait for later?"* she thought.

Her right hand began softly caressing the inside of her warm thighs. Her forefinger and thumb found her erect clitoris between the vee in her outstretched legs and began the rhythmic dance of caressing it and rubbing it faster and faster.

"Oh, this is just the sexy reward I need now," she gasped. She plunged a finger inside her wet vagina.

Her fingers continued their rhythmic dance on her stiff clitoris as the tension built. Her right hand rose to her breasts, plucked at her nipples, and then back between her thighs riding in and out of her lubricated vagina.

Finally, the rhythm of her left hand over her erect clitoris and her right-hand plunging in and out of her sensitive vagina matched the pace she really needed. Clutching her thighs, she began to tremble with that wonderful climax one can achieve when satisfying oneself. As the tremors receded, she slowed the pace of caressing herself.

Finally, she stopped and, holding her breasts, she said, "Well, back to the shower to clean up before the victory dinner."

Looking down at her copper mound, she promises, "Yes, dear sweet lips, I'll be back."

Chapter 2 Getting Even Is The Best Reward

Shelbi's plan to get revenge was warrior perfect.

She had worked out with her fighting coach exactly how to take a 6-foot 5 man down. Not gracefully but quickly face down onto the cold hard floor.

Shelbi had done her reconnaissance work and carefully studied Brendenn's daily pattern in the school. She knew every other night he went to the exercise gym along with his 3 companions. As a leader he was aggressive and always finish his power program before they had.

That's when he would be alone.

He would walk down the narrow grey corridor, turned down the second corridor toward the change room. Alone. Unfocused. Unaware of the danger.

Shelbi did a lightweight workout managing her adrenaline but warming up her muscles. At exactly the right moment she saw him leaving the gym. She darted out the second entrance and around into the corridor waiting for him.

As planned, he walked around the corner rubbing his sweaty neck with the yellow towel, his right hand extended.

Swiftly her right hand grabbed his right wrist starting him in motion as she squatted down and used her left leg to knock his legs out from underneath them. As he spun towards the hard floor, she turned him over quickly. She wanted him to land on his chest to take his wind out not damaging his head.

It went exactly as planned.

Shelbi had his arm pinned up behind him. Her knee tight in his crotch and her elbow pressed against his neck. She heard rather than saw a slight commotion around her. Brendenn whispered one-word, "Katonna."

Shelbi leaned over and whispered in his ear, "Brendenn you lizard I want you to say, Shelbi I'm sorry."

She applied a little more pressure to his right arm increasing the pain.

"Now!" said Shelbi.

Calmly but very clearly Brendenn said, "Shelbi I'm sorry."

Shelbi jumped up dancing on the balls of her feet. "Brendenn, remember I can do this again at any time. Just leave my buns alone!"

With that she left him sitting on the floor and darted off down the corridor racing towards her room.

The plan had work perfectly.

As she entered her room's she started dancing around and saying, "Yes, the plan worked. Yes! Yes!"

Her joyous dance was interrupted by the chiming of her message com.

Looking at the name Commander Rebecca Julie Fornia she paused and quickly answered it. "Cadet MacPhadden here sir."

The message was short and simple from the commander. "My office, now."

Drat. There must've been a hidden camera she hadn't noted in her plan.

As she hurried to the commander's office her mind reviewed the alternative explanation she had developed. She needed to explained to the commander she was merely defending her honor.

As she walked into the cold blue office of the commander, she noticed the second in command was sitting at his workstation. He looked at her and said, "Cadet MacPhadden please go right in." No emotion. No smile. But not stern.

Shelbi walked in to the office executed a smart salute. "Cadet MacPhadden as requested sir!"

Commander Rebecca Fornia looked at Shelbi and smiled. "Please have a seat, Cadet MacPhadden."

The commander rose out of her chair picking up her tablet and started to walk out of the office.

As she passed Shelbi she merely commented, "I'll be back."

Shelbi sat in the chair, puzzled. She had expected a skin flailing reprimand.

Moments later the second-in-command walked in and sat down in the chair beside her. Samuel Arthur McMahon was a seasoned war veteran. He ran the commander's office by the official rules book. He not only used the book he wrote much of it.

He smiled slightly at Shelbi. "In a moment Cadet Shelbi I'm going to leave the room. A door is going to open. We would like it if you went through the door into the adjoining room. As you know there are a number of secure rooms throughout the Academy. This is one of the highest security rooms. No cameras.

No listening devices. No penetration possible by listening devices. Please enjoy the conversation with the person in that room." As he finished his short monologue he rose out of the chair, walked out of the room and swiftly shut the office door.

Just as Samuel had said part of the bookcase slid back revealing a door. Shelbi walked up and noted no door handle just a hand scan on the wall. Putting her right hand on the scanner the door opened. She walked into the room.

And there he was.

That lizard Brendenn sitting in a chair.

As she entered the room he immediately stood up and bowed. "Shelbi Elizabeth Mary MacPhadden. I formally apologize for my ungentlemanly actions in the past. I would appreciate it if you would accept my sincere apology as a gentleman. I would also appreciate the time to explain my crude actions."

Shelbi was clearly taken aback and slightly shocked. She had not anticipated a formal apology.

Shelbi smiled, "Brendenn Armstrong Michael Corzann, yes, I accept your apology. And I would really like to understand what the pipe was going on!"

Brandon gestured for her to take the black chair. When she had sat down, he sat in the blue chair beside her.

"Shelbi you know the planet that I come from, but what many don't know is my title is really Prince Royal. I am the leader of half of my home planet. The three people that are with me are warrior trainees just like you. But there also my designated protectors. Sabrinna has grown up with me. The other two have been with me since my tenth birthday."

Shelbi squinted her eyes slightly and looked at him. She was processing all this information.

"So, when I took you down, they could've ripped me off of you?" Shelbi asked.

"Absolutely," Brendenn said, "if I had not said the one word, they would've taken you down and perhaps done some damage. I can't afford to have that happen."

"I don't understand your comment you can't afford to have it happen," Shelbi said with puzzlement.

"Shelbi when I first saw you, I felt a wave of energy flow over me and I reacted. The first thing my hand came in contact with unfortunately was your right backside cheek. I felt a slight trickle of energy as I held your beautiful shape. Every time I go by you it's almost a compulsion to touch you and feel that energy flow. I don't know what it does. I don't know how it works. But something in my brain says it's important to understand. I just never had the nerve to talk to you about it."

"What do you mean energy?" Asked Shelbi.

"It's hard to explain. My companions asked me to stop or talk to you. I just haven't had the gumption until now. I will ask you now. I would like to continue to explore what this energy feeling is. Or, I will stop touching you I promise."

"So, is this a sexual thing you're getting all excited and trying to be a man?" Shelbi said emphatically.

"No, it's not sexual. It's something that rolls up my spine and into my head. It's almost like I can see and feel something differently. I don't know what it means is. I never touched you long enough to find out."

"So, you don't find me sexy!" Shelbi demanded.

"No, no, no that's not what I mean," Brendenn stammered, "on the contrary I find you amazingly sexy. With those wonderful curvy hips and wild red hair, it's all I can do to keep my lips from caressing your cheeks, kissing down your neck and holding you tightly. But when I touch you it's a completely different feeling. It's like you're a conduit of some sort of energy. I really don't understand it. It's confusing. I really wish it was a simple as sex."

Shelbi was quiet for a moment and Brendenn allowed her the time. He could clearly see she was processing and thinking.

She looked at the Prince differently now. She began to sense this was bigger than just grabbing her rear cheek. The entrepreneurial warrior in her really wanted to explore more.

"Brendenn I'd like to explore this. There's something here neither of us understand. Now you mention it when you touch me there is a sensation I also feel. It is either really important or just your hormones gone wild. I also wouldn't mind a little sex while we do the exploring!" She said with a laugh.

Brendenn smiled and quickly moved to her chair and gathering her in his arm. He kissed her right cheek. He kissed her left cheek with his warm hot lips. Then he moved down her neck one kiss at a time.

As he was kissing her Shelbi's hands were roaming up-and-down is muscular broad back.

Then Brendenn stepped back. They both had felt the sexual urges rising but also something else playing around the edges. They weren't sure what it was but it was interesting.

Shelbi made the move this time. She embraced Brendenn crushing her soft round breasts against his chiseled manly chest. She could feel at the front of his pants, his eager manhood starting to respond to the sexual part of what they were doing. The semi-hardness poking at the softness of her belly.

As Brendenn lean down to kiss her waiting lips, the door chime sounded. Brendenn stepped back from Shelbi, placing his hands over his hardness and looked up as the door opened.

Sabrinna stood in the doorway. Calmly she said, "Brendenn is it yes or is it no?"

Brendenn looked at Sabrinna and smiled. "Exploration Shelbi project is ago!"

Sabrinna stepped in the room and Shelbi could see the two other companions standing behind her. Sabrinna put her hand on the inside sensitive scanner plate and the door closed with the three of them in the room.

She walked over to Shelbi and pushed Brendenn out of the way so she could sit in chair front of Shelbi. "I know that Brendenn has apologized. Let me tell you as a friend we have no idea why he acts this way towards you. He truly is a gentleman. I know you find that hard to understand, but hopefully as you get to know all of us you really see this is completely out of place for him."

She looked directly at Brendenn then turned back to Shelbi, "Each time he grabbed you I gave them a shot in the arm. He has a good-sized bruise that he is earned. It's one of the reasons we needed to put this to an end before I started to do some real damage to him. And believe me I was at that point where I would've taken him down if you hadn't."

With that short speech Shelbi felt she truly had found another friend at the Academy.

"Brendenn I'm not sure all that you are up to in this room," Sabrinna said with a smile on her face, "but the second I opened the door I felt an energy flow up my back into my mind and I could see things a little clearer. I'm not sure what that means?"

Shelbi then glanced back and forth between the two of them and said, "Yes, I felt an energy flow that wasn't just sexual it was something else. I don't know what to think of it?"

Sabrinna looked at Brendenn and continued, "It's not there now. But there was definitely something different in my head after I walked in this room. I don't think I was just imagining it."

The three of them decided to explore it further but not tell anyone about it.

Forces were thus set in motion that none of them would've ever thought about in the room. Good forces that would ultimately would try to change their lives. And bad forces that would ultimately try to end their lives.

Chapter 3 Pain and Pleasure

Shelbi awoke fully aware it was her 6-month physical exam day.

"At first, I thought this was a waste of time. But after the rugby game incident I now really understand how important it is," She thought.

With over 27 different species and more than 250 planets that students were selected from, the chances of alien cross disease happening were high. The Academy work hard to make sure that the various diseases were not passed on from cadet to cadet.

Shelbi had been at the Academy a little over 3 months. She had joined the rugby league almost as soon as she arrived at the Academy. The once-a-week games were very physical and gave her an opportunity to stay fit, think about strategy and have some rough exciting fun.

She came back from the game with a couple of scratches on her left hand as well as multiple bruises. After she showered and was preparing for bed, she noticed her left-hand seem to have small blue scales around one of the cuts.

She thought nothing of it.

As she sat down at her computer to fill in her Personal Journal for the day, she noticed the scales seem to have cover her hand up to her wrist. She also felt a little stiffening in her left hand.

"I did have the ball tucked in there when I got tackled really hard. My left hand got slammed into the ground hard several times. That's probably what it is."

After an hour she noticed that her hand and wrist now were covered with tiny blue almost incandescent scales. They felt soft but also took any sensation out of her skin. The Cadets had been warned in their pre-briefing and several other times if the experience any health changes go immediately to the medical center.

She changed into a casual uniform and walked out to the moving sidewalk that took her to the medical center. As she walked in the entrance, she put her scaly hand down on a scanning device, which immediately let out a low pitch alert.

The nurse on duty jumped out of her chair and commanded, "Cadet MacPhadden stand perfectly still. Medical attention will be brought to you immediately!"

Shelbi did as commanded standing at attention. A door on the left wall opened and two interns in med suits pushing a covered gurney walked toward her. They opened it up and helped her inside and closed it quickly. She was taken to a sterile room where a doctor and a nurse, both in med suits, walked in and open the clear cover.

The doctor took a quick look at the scales now up her arm past her elbow. Immediately he slapped a med pad on the outside of her arm. Then lifting up her arm one inside her wrist.

The nurse took out a strip dressing which was wound around Shelbi's hand, her wrist and upper arm past her elbow. It automatically tightened not unlike a tourniquet but not quite as hard.

"You'll be here for a minimum of 4 hours while this medication takes effect. You'll then need 6 days of treatment to make sure this doesn't recur." The nurse said.

Then the doctor asked questions. "What were you doing tonight that cause this injury? Who were you with?"

Shelbi explained, "I was part of a rugby game tonight. There were 2 cadets from Retaw world. I didn't think anything of it."

The doctor didn't comment and appeared to be slightly unfocused as his lips moved. He returned his gaze to Shelbi and said, "I just requested security review the game tape. We will find the two cadets and will make sure they receive the necessary treatment. This is not a big issue just a minor inconvenience. But it must be treated. If the scales had moved on to your torso you could've been here for several days of treatment. Do you have any questions?"

"With this recur? Will it limit anything I can do? Is this an issue that will be on my record?"

The doctor smiled, "Your treatment tonight will cure you this particular time. It's also working with Nano bots in your bloodstream to remove anything that might linger for the future. Having caught it so soon it will not limit anything you do. Yes, it will go on your record as a medical item but only as a medical item. It's not a discipline issue or anything that would limit your career. In fact, it's an enhancement."

Shelbi process the information then asked another question, "How could it be an enhancement?"

"The fact that you received the infection but your body and existing Nano bots slowed the spread is a big positive for the future. It means that many diseases that would impact you off world may be contained or controllable by your exiting nanobots."

With that the doctor and nurse both smiled. The nurse said, "Relax and enjoy the next couple of hours. We will turn the lights down so you can have asleep."

Shelbi remembered the incident as she got dressed for the six-month medical knowing that they were very important.

She arrived promptly at 09:00 for her medical appointment. She stepped into the room and looked through the crystal window at the technician, nurse and doctor. She knew what to do. She stripped off her shirt, pants, underwear, boots, and socks. Then carefully folded them on the tray jutting out of the wall. It then moved into the wall and she knew they were all being sterilized.

She stepped on the footprints on the floor which opened to show she was standing on a grid. A clear tube descended out of the wall and surrounded her entire body. She put her fingertips on the holders beside her forming a vee with her arms. She closed her eyes and felt the soft rain of thousands of Nano bots as they were sprayed from the top of her head to the bottom of her legs. Underneath Nano bots were sprayed on the soles of her feet.

They would send back all sorts of information so that her entire body had been scanned covering almost every cell of her skin, hair, eyelids and all parts of her body.

As a ring lower down releasing the Nano bots it felt like 1,000 tiny fingers softly caressing her skin. Her nipples tented.

She really had to focus because it felt very sexual in nature. And she knew the next part would definitely be sensual.

The ring moved over her a second time warmly washing over skin to make sure all the Nano bots had been washed through the grid in the floor for analysis.

She put her arms down at her side but spread her legs open. A small device extended out of the tube in front of her looking very much like a slim dildo. The top of the device was a cup which push slightly in between her thighs and against her warm vagina lips. It pushed them open ever so slightly again collecting data at the same time.

The center part of the device touched her nether lips as Shelbi sucked in her breath at the sensual feeling. The warmth of the device and its self-lubrication began as it slowly inserted itself into her vagina.

As part of her initial medical Shelbi had identified that she had been sexually active. Which meant she was not a virgin.

This device was initially gathering data inside her vagina to make sure she hadn't collected any sexual diseases.

As it sat fully inserted inside, she had the urge to push against it. She had talked to other female cadets and knew they all had the same sensual perception.

"It's so damn slow-going in," Jennifer said. The other cadets laughed. "Yes, it must've been design to give us some pleasure to offset the discomfort," Jasmine said.

Shelbi waited while the heat increased in her vagina as the instrumentation did multiple inspections and gathered multiple samples.

Then just when she thought she couldn't take much more without caressing herself it slowly began to descend out of her channel. As it went it sprayed the special lubricant that would protect her from all known sexual diseases.

The tube descended and her clothes appeared along with a large yellow towel. As she dried her body off, she thought, *"I can't wait to get back to my room tonight. I really need to take advantage of this sensation and build on the pleasure that this has created."*

Chapter 4 Strategy Project

Loose lips sink ships. An old Earth slogan still used to keep cadets aware of enemy danger when going on leave in off world ports.

Tight rear shifts career. Shelbi laughed out loud as she thought, *"There's a new slogan."* With Brendenn grabbing her backside and then her taking him down she had shifted her focus for her keystone paper for this academic year.

As she walked toward the commander's office, in charge of strategy training, she thought back to how she had started this journey for the term paper she was about to pitch.

In talking to Brendenn, she been fascinated by his planets culture. They've been known as the warriors that could not be beaten. While this was a culture that went back over 1,000 years and war really wasn't a big issue today their cultural history still protected them.

She talked briefly with the strategy commander about her thoughts on a term paper and he had encouraged her. He mentioned that his first strategy term paper had been on the Zecondain battle. It had been fought by one of Brendenn's ancestors. Having been outnumbered almost 3 to 1, their brilliant strategy had not only subdued but had beaten the enemy with a third of the loss of life.

As she talked more to Brendenn and the instructor and did some research she found a legend. A group of bronze warriors drove the strategy that help them beat many enemies. The legend was the bronze warriors were naked on the command bridge. Shelbi felt she really needed to explore and find out the real parts of the legend. All legends have real parts it's finding them that's the important key to their usefulness.

On Saturday afternoons the commander opened his office to those who wanted to have one-on-one discussions.

She reached the commander's office and palm the scanner to notify him she was there.

This is more than just a one-on-one discussion as Shelbi wanted to pitch her keystone term paper. If it was rejected, she had to start over and find a new topic.

The door opened and she walked into the front office noting the support staff was not there. The commander's voice floated out of his office, "Cadet Shelbi. Come in and let's have some tea."

Shelbi was slightly tense and as she entered the office gave him a salute. She held it till he looked up. A smile crossed his face, "At ease cadet Shelbi. This is really a conversation as friends not formal."

"Thank you, sir. I have my strategic keynote term paper outline on this wand for you." She handed him the electronic wand and, he placed it on his desk.

"Why don't you just tell me what you would like your keynote term paper to be. We'll have a discussion and then I can look at the formal documents."

Shelbi had thought about what to say knowing that this was the style of the Commander instructor. She had decided that talking about Brendenn grabbing her butt was probably not a good idea. But the conversation she'd had with Brendenn and Sabrinna around the energy concept was safe ground.

As she spoke, she warmed to the subject and her passion for both strategy and uncovering the legend could clearly be felt by the commander.

Shelbi paused, "Do you have any questions sir? Or do you need more information?"

The commander smiled. "Shelbi I can see you are really passionate about this and want to investigate it. I'm also interested. As you know I did my first strategy paper on the Zecondain battle. It looked at the strategies they developed. They were brilliant. In fact, many of the basic battle strategies that we have today come directly from this culture. At the same time the legend of the bronze warriors is fascinating. Naked people running around on a command ship seems very bizarre."

The commander picked up the wand Shelbi had given him and inserted it into the slot in the top of his desk. It glowed connecting to the virtual screen that popped up on his left side. He keyed in a few words and a coded number.

"Shelbi, I don't need to read this at the moment. You have done an excellent job outlining your keynote term paper. I've logged your paper and also provided a special code that you can use whenever you're accessing information. It gives you a higher priority to find data then your cadet level allows. It also gives you access to the classic manuscript archives. I know my paper from 55 years ago is in there. Also, other papers I researched are in there. This code will allow you to access that. Let me know when you want to go and I'll book the first appointment. Once you've logged in and then set up the achieve security clearance you can go at your own time."

Shelbi was fascinated that he had simply approved her term paper on her verbal patch. "I like to go tomorrow afternoon commander. I am really keen to gather more information."

With several keystrokes the commander accessed the schedule and noted that 3 o'clock tomorrow afternoon was open. He logged in Shelbi with her new security code and his security code.

"Shelbi I'm not sure if you're aware but in the archives, there are electronic material plus there's actual paper documents. You will have to wear antistatic gloves when working with the electronic documents. If you work with the paper documents, they have special white cotton gloves which you would wear over the static gloves. I know it's a bit awkward but this material is priceless and we guarded it very carefully."

Shelbi had been aware of some of the special things that had to happen working in the archives but since it was unusual for a second-year cadet to get out access to it she hadn't spent much time learning about it.

Shelbi thanked him for his support and left. Thus, her journey started that could end lives and save others.

Chapter 5 Armour Titillating Mistake

Shelbi walked into the year two cadets assigned locker room in the robotic warrior building. In just a few moments she was about to be strapped into 350 pounds of blue bullet deflecting steel. Armed with lasers and armor piercing bullets she was prepared to continue her learning how to survive, adapt or kill as needed.

Walking out onto the loading area floor in her white skin suite, she came to the armoured suit she had been assigned. She stepped out of her shoes and placed her feet on the foot imprints on the floor. Her earpiece came alive. "Cadet MacPhadden, are you ready?"

"Yes, control I am ready." Shelbi had been through 76 hours of in class training. She had been through 92 hours of lab mechanical training. She had learned to take apart a suit and put it back together again. She had learned how to do minor repairs that may happen in a combat zone.

Seconds later a spiral wheel emerged out of the floor behind her as a pair of blue steel boots emerged in front of her. She stepped into the boots as the wheel surrounded her and began to assemble all the mechanical parts of her blue body armor.

Moments later she felt slightly claustrophobic as the faceplate lowered and she was sealed inside. She could feel the foam interior expand to support her body up the back of her legs roll up over her curvy hips, upper torso and finally over her breasts. Something didn't feel quiet, right? But nothing seemed out of place and Shelbi decide to investigate it later.

The voice in her ear continued, "Cadet Shelbi you are cleared for the Samuel Dickerson beginner's trail. See you in 3 hours. Be safe out there."

She stepped forward tentatively feeling slightly off-balance. As she strode out of the warehouse onto the red tarmac, she felt confident as her the balance returned. She walked down to the beginner's trail and saw 50 steps that she had to climb up.

"Put your right hand on the rail for at least the first 25 steps so you get the feeling." The female instructor in her ear piece said.

Shelbi wasn't sure about this but decided that instructions were meant to be followed. Questioning instructions could get people killed.

She reached out and began the climb. Immediately she saw why you needed to grasp the railing as she felt a little unbalanced. Halfway up she had the rhythm and dropped her hand from the rail and kept moving.

Somewhere in the back of her mind something wasn't quite right with the suit. Still, she could not put her finger on it.

Having reached the top of the stairs she now saw the trail curved around the side of an artificial mountain. As she walked around the corner, she saw a large tree blocking the trail. She began to think about the best approach to this.

"With the power in the suit I could simply lifted the tree up, walking it over to the canyons edge and throw it out into the chasm. However, that would use a lot of energy early in my practice round. I could cut it apart with the laser and then walk through. Again, that would take a lot of energy. If I use Newton's law of the lever, I could simply pick up the large end and tip it over the edge."

As she got closer to the log and inspected it, she saw the small indentation cut into a rock that would form a cradle. She went to the large end, rolled it onto the rock and tipped it up. It slid off the rock and the chasm easily. *"Nicely done,"* She thought.

Shelbi continued on up the path and moments later came around a corner just as her screen beeped, a hail of enemy bullets met her right side and she quickly stepped back.

She hadn't been focusing on the screen or she would've seen her advanced radar noted the enemy. Lesson learned. No more daydreaming and checking out the landscape. Make sure you're focusing on messages on the screen as part of what you're doing.

She now knew exactly where the enemy was hiding. She said the command to arm up her bullets and stepped around the corner firing. Her aim was a little low. *"This must've been set up for a larger person than I am, the sites firing low,"* She thought to herself.

Quickly she took out the target. Then she checked her ammunition. She had used up 8% of her bullets.

"I'll definitely have to do better in the future that's way too much ammunition early on in both this practice round or in a real-world battle. I'll have to suit up and go to the target range and work on that."

She continued on the trail and once again the scanner popped up *enemy high in tree*. She continued walking and as she rounded the corner dropped to her knee shooting up at the target that the screen showed. She then looked at the shots on this exercise. Usage 3% of bullets.

"Much better. Watching the screen and setting up the target before the action is important."

She continued and came to a steep incline.

"Run with as much speed as you can exert to the top of the mountain. The object of this exercise is to help you understand speed, balance and the results of exerting yourself." Instructions in her ear helped her understand exactly what was about to transpire.

She turned and pumped as hard as she could as she sprinting up the hill. With the suit assist she moved over the hundred yards in less than 6 seconds. When she reached the top, she felt the exertion.

She also discovered what bothered her.

Shelbi laughed to herself when she realized the suit had probably been warned by a male previously. The cup protector that covered the front of their manhood was still erect. The foam padding was press down on her sensitive area. The movement especially the running up the hill, had sent tremors through her suit causing the manhood cup to rub against her sensitive clitoris.

"Great now I am going to be super horny when I finish! A small price to pay to save the world."

"Run down the hill as fast as you can quickly turning right at the corner. The objective is to understand the balance and what will happen as your momentum carries you forward." More instructions in her ear gave her pause to think.

She ran down the hill as fast as she could. About halfway down she realized she was going to do a face plant. She rolled to her right side and ended up falling on her shoulder doing 3 or 4 somersaults before coming to a stop.

"Interesting." She was going to have to learn how to run down a hill actually leaning backwards in order

to avoid this. Additionally, she was going to have to learn how to roll and end up planting her feet so she's standing up. She now began to realize why it would take at least 3 times through this course before you are qualified to go to the medium effort Reese L'Engle course.

As Shelbi move further down the course, she now was a little over 2 hours into it. She came across a river and a crossing area.

"This looks too easy. I'm certain there's a trick if I simply walk on to the path." She thought to herself as her mind began to play out different scenarios.

She picked up 3 stones. She threw the first one and saw it plopped down in the water. She threw it had little further and noticed that disappeared quite quickly.

"I'll bet there's a hole that would swallow up my suit. I know it's waterproof but it might be difficult to get out of a hole.

If this was the enemy and they had set a trap this is where you could end it all."

She decided while it would take a little longer to go north as that was the way the water was flowing. Any holes that were dug would fill in with sediment as the stream pushed the dirt down into them.

Shelbi cautiously walked across and found she could find firm sand for walking. By the middle of the stream, she was up to her waist. As she continued on, she came to a slight slope and emerged out of the water. Later she would learn that yes, it was a trick. She would actually have fallen in a hole. With the sifting sand at the bottom, she would've had great difficulty getting out of the hole.

At just under 2 ½ hours she came to the end of the trail. She walked onto the tarmac and back to the space where she had gotten into the suit. She backed in to the rack and put her feet on the markings on the floor. Immediately her screen began downloading all the information her suite contains. The suit had been monitoring her blood pressure, heart rate, and other vital signs. It also noted each one of the tasks, the time it took to perform and how she performed it. The energy used, rounds of ammunition and other key factors were also collected. This would all be analyzed and report provided to her tomorrow morning.

She knew in real time; data had been sent in case she got in trouble. The Academy had the sense to know that new cadets could often get in trouble. They wanted to make sure that if there was trouble, they learned from that trouble before it took their life.

The wheel again emerged and began removing parts of the blue suit.

When she was down to her tight-fitting skin suit, she stepped back into her boots and walked back to the locker room to put on her uniform. Two and half hours in the suit constant gentle rubbing over clitoris. She couldn't wait to get in the shower and take care of this sensation she had. It was enough she was on a high from having been in the suit for the first time, traveling the course and doing what she thought was very good.

She walked down the corridor to her private room Sheila Harvard stepped out of her room.

"Well Shelbi how was it?" Sheila said.

Shelbi launched into a brief discussion talking at a quick pace.

Sheila held up her hand, "You forgot the man cup. Did I not tell you about the man cup?"

Shelbi remained silent.

"Go, go to the shower enjoy yourself!" Sheila smiled to Shelbi turned and hurried toward her room.

Walking into her room she took off her boots. Then she removed her skin suit and put it in the fresher and almost bolted into the shower. She slammed her hand on the water button and jumped in the shower.

She felt the warm spray covering her body and starting to slice off the sweat that had accumulated inside the suit.

She began by soaping her neck and her shoulders. She then lathered up using both hands one on each breast.

Because of the agitation on her clitoris, she found that her nipples were perky and had been massaged by the foam in the suit adding to her sensations.

She ran the soap over her belly and around her back. As she caressed the soap over the curve of her bottom, she felt the wetness between her thighs building that was not the running warm water. She bent over and began to soap her legs starting at her ankles. By the time her hands were running up the inside of her leg she knew she had to give in to the demands of her begging clitoris.

She ran the soap into her copper mound and created a good solid lather. Then using your other hand, she dropped the lather down between her thighs.

Her fingers slid across her erect nub and slightly parted her vagina lips. They too were tingling and looking for caresses and attention.

She rubbed her finger up and down the lips of her vagina lips. The lubrication gave her rhythm that she could keep up with comfort and build excitement.

She moved her finger up and down her other hand came began to rub the inside of her thighs. Then it moved up to moving back and forth across her eager swollen clitoris.

Shelbi wanted to continue the sensation and was not yet ready to come.

She took her hand away from her clitoris and pushed her middle finger into the hot channel of her vagina. While the soap had washed off, she had her own self lubrication that allowed her finger to slide in and out easily.

Her other hand started to knead her breasts and palm her nipples. She plucked tenderly at the right nipple. Then moved over to the left nipple. Then began a rhythm of plucking as her fingers slid in and out.

She grasped her breast as the tension continued and caressed herself with eagerness. This slight stretching rubbed the sides of her warm channel.

She moved her fingers out of the channel and as the warm water splashed on her back began to work on her clitoris in earnest. Her hand clutched her breast and applied some pressure to her nipple.

Her fingers sped up as they move back and forth across her sensitive clitoris. She could feel the tension building in her legs and across her belly. At last, the momentum built and she came in one spectacular leg quivering climax.

Her fingers moved across her tender bud and buried themselves deep insider to move back and forth in the warm channel. At last, they emerged and rubbed the side of her thighs. She had let go of her breasts and put both her hands on the top of her thighs.

The trembling stopped and she felt what a wonderful climax. It was well worth the two and half hours on the trail with the armour titillation.

"However next time I'll have to concentrate on the trail and not so much the shower at the end!"

Chapter 6 Warrior Assignment Insights

Shelbi stepped off the cargo ramp of the jet cargo plane and began her freefall in the planet's blue atmosphere.

After freefalling for 2,000 feet, she activated the silver wing glider and leveled out heading towards her target drop spot two miles away.

If she landed within 100 feet of her drop zone target, she would set an exercise record. Awards were nice but she was more interested in understanding her physical limits and how the silver wing glider works. She didn't see the point in experimenting in the middle of battle. Better to know what you could do and what it could do before the enemy was involved.

She scanned the area as she glided over the forest knowing that hunting animals below wanted to attack other living beings for food.

For the next eighteen days she would be tracking through the wilderness seeing if she could survive off the land. Her target the WPE Summit compound. Shelbi knew that only 40% of all second-year cadets doing the survival exercise made it to the summit. She also knew that only 62% of all the final year grads made it. She was going to make sure she made it her first time.

Her mind reviewed the drop zone she was aiming for. While there were still many high trees, she was gliding over she knew there was an area she could drop down and glide to a perfect landing. She also had identified a secondary zone at 1.93 miles. Even that would help set a record. Most cadets took a glide of 2 miles or less before stepping on the terrafirma.

She trusted the research she done and even though she was getting closer and closer to the tall trees she knew there would be a break soon. Just as she had planned, she spotted the break as her toes began to brush the limbs of the treetops.

Slightly off her glide vector she shifted her body and course corrected. Gliding across the grassy area she pulled up within 10 feet of her target point. *"Excellent job,"* she thought.

She unstrapped the wings and attached her helmet to the glider. Folding the wings, she activated the recall button. Someone would come in the next 24 hours and retrieved them.

The heat at 42°C immediately cause a sheen of perspiration to cover her body. Her sunglasses help to cut the glare from the sun. She was glad she had used a sunshield cream to cover those parts of her body there were exposed.

Shelbi did a quick inventory of what she had on. Wearing hiking boots and special socks to absorb perspiration, a knife strapped to her thigh, her athletic shorts and top that would catch the breeze and allow the moisture to escape, and the microchip under her arm.

The microchip was the recall button that once pressed would activate the search and rescue people to come and gather her. This was a test training exercise but the Academy didn't really want to lose warriors who push themselves too hard. In fact, failure to achieve the goal of reaching the summit was not actually considered a failure. It's how you had move forward. What you had accomplished? What led to you pushing the button to be rescued?

Shelbi oriented her mind to the route she had mapped out. She began to walk forward at a reasonable pace. Since the adrenaline of the drop-in glide was still pounding in her she knew one of the rookie mistakes was to start off to fast and tire too soon on day one. She had a set number of miles she needed to cover and wanted to make sure she reached her mileage goals each and every day. Her Fitbit X would keep track of the miles.

She saw it was getting near sunset. She found a small clearing. She unsheathed their knife and walked around till she found the sting bush. Its large thorns were needed to help her create a protective ring. She went back to where she was going to camp for the night and used her knife to dig in the soil to create a fire pit. She then roamed around and found several fallen trees that were dry enough to start a good fire.

When she gathered more than she felt she needed she went back and started to attack the sting bush.

She knew this was the dangerous part. Despite being careful she was pricked again and again by the strong needle-sharp thorns. That's sent small trails of blood trickling down her legs and her arms. Shelbi knew this would attract danger.

The werewolves are the most dangerous part of the mission. Their eyes could see in the dark. They didn't hunt during the day because the fierce sun hurt their eyes. At night they could smell blood miles away.

Their eyes allowed them to see the slightest movement of a leaf on a tree or a flick of the eyelid of their prey.

Before she finished her sting bush circle, she lit the fire. Immediately it was reflected in pairs of golden orbs circling her. She knew she had to work quickly or she would be in difficulty.

She had cut a limb off of an oak tree was about 6 feet in length and 2 inches in diameter. She sharpened the tip and stuck it in the fire creating an even harder charred tip.

Shelbi had gathered a dozen milky weed pods. Sticking one on the end of her spear and lighting it then placing it by the fire could serve as a deterrent to the werewolves. They found the smell noxious.

She finished the sting bush ring and sat down thinking, *"It's time for nutrition."* She had 12 tubes of water and 12 nutrition bars. Not enough for eighteen days but enough to supplement her after she added her own fresh water, meat and plants.

After consuming one nutrition bar and water tube she sat down and cross the spear across her lap. The milk pod was already attached to the end and the fire was blazing away. After several hours she had lulled herself into the feeling she had outsmarted the werewolf's but instinct saved her.

She heard the crunching of the Wolf as it raced towards her and launched into the air over the sting bush barricade. She had quickly lit the milky weed pod and as he descended on her she crouched and drove her spear and into its opening mouth. At 210 pounds its velocity carried him forward and knocked her to the ground bruising ribs on her right side. She quickly flips him over and drove the spear through the back of his skull. Pulling out her knife she severed the head and used the flaming milk weed pod stick threw it back over the barricade.

Quickly she cut off each of the legs and threw it in different directions and then picking up the eighty-pound body and flung it over the side. Unfortunately, not very far. Immediately flickering eyes moved forward. She saw many werewolves grab the carcass and drag it into the wilderness. She hoped that might satisfy their hunger. She knew it probably wouldn't since their whole being was driven to hunt at night.

Several of the wolves got adventurous and were quite near the prickle bushes circling her. She lit milkweed pods and threw them out them over the barricade. The fifth one actually landed on a beast back and set its fur on fire. It raced into the woods. A torch followed by several of its companions who saw their dinner was being roasted.

With less than an hour to sunrise and the fire low she heard them rustling around and could see the flicker of their pairs of yellow eyes. She turned and lit a milkweed pod just as she heard one flyover despite turning quickly it landed on its side.

It was a young Wolf but it made a mistake, a costly mistake. It growled a victory growl and slowly stalked toward Shelbi. She grasped the rock that she'd had around the fire and hurled it with all her might hitting it on its head stunning it. That allowed her to grab her spear and drive it into its skull killing it.

This one was light enough for her to throw it over the barricade and watch as members of the pack grabbed it and dragged it away tearing hunks of flesh off it as they went.

Finally, the sun rays broke through the forest trees.

Shelbi looked at the damage to her legs from the thorns. She took off her top and examined her ribs carefully. None were broken just bruised. The ugly blue and purple bruise was beginning to show.

Knowing she was safe in the sunlight she curled up and went to sleep for two hours.

She had expected one night of this challenge with the werewolves. Not the first night. She was slightly behind schedule but she would catch it up.

She knew with their intelligence that they would note that they had not defeated her and would probably leave her alone looking for easier prey to take down.

Using her spear, she moved the sting Bush aside and began her journey on day 2. She used some grass to try and get some of the dried blood off her arms, hands, and shorts. She knew it would be for 5 days before she could get to water and wash properly. However, covered in blood of the werewolf would actually deter certain other predators.

She cut off a third of her power bar and drank half of one of her the water tubes, ready to move out for the day.

Today she needed to find food of her own to save rations for later in her adventure.

Chapter 7 Naked Waterfall Washing

Shelbi emerged from the dense forest edge on day 5 and sighted her target. A thousand yards to her left she could see the mist rising from the Amber River waterfall as it fell 200 feet into the mini lake.

She made her way to the edge and sank down on the jutting rock in the heat of the afternoon. She was 3 hours ahead of schedule. This would allow her the luxury to wash her clothes, her body and perhaps enjoy some self-pleasure.

Carefully climbing down the red marbled rocks at the edge of the lake, she came to the waterfall and as planned follow the trail behind it into the alcove. She took off her backpack and laid it on the ground along with her hat.

She sat down and pulled the green aquwa leaves from the pocket in the side of her backpack. Her studies showed the sap from these large leaves combined with the water would create a soapy substance. She can use it to wash the sweat and grim of five days in the jungle. She could also use it to wash her sweat stained clothes.

She undid the laces of her brown Academy Pro hiking boots and took them off sitting them behind the alcove so the waterfall would not splash on them. She shed the rest of her clothes, pulling the other dirty ones out of her pack and took a quick inventory. She had two T-shirts, two pairs of grey socks, two pairs of plain beige underwear, one beige bra, one brown bra, one pair khaki shorts and one green long sleeve shirt. All sweat and dirt stained from her journey through the forest in the muggy hot weather.

She dove in the water and just enjoyed it washing over her naked body. Stepping out onto the beach she broke open the stem of the aquwa leaf and tripped the green sap into the palm of her hand. Lathering it up she soaped her entire torso enjoying getting rid of the grit and grime.

She started rubbing it around her neck and across her shoulders. Then over her ample breasts realizing that she wanted to do some more playful things with them.

Then she walked to the edge of the water as she continued to lather across her belly and her back. As she applied more sap to her palm and added water, she began to lather her backside bringing her soapy hands around to the front caressing up the side of her hot thighs. A little more sap and she began to work the copper triangle above her vagina. Then Shelbi began applying soap between her thighs. She realized how much she was enjoying it and she really needed to reward herself after she finished washing her clothes.

One more time she dove from rock into the water feeling the coolness wash over her skin. Coining out of the lake she grabbed the remaining bunch of leaves and walked around to a set of rocks near the water's edge. Looking at the smooth grey and red surface she knew it would be a great place to dryer her cloths. She then proceeded to wash her underwear and bras. She laid them out in the hot afternoon sun on the hot red rocks. She continued working on the rest of her clothes and spreading them on the rocks to dry.

Shelbi laid down on the rock beside her clothes and let the sun dry her body. The heat of the afternoon sun on her breasts began to excite Shelbi. The heat on her legs, thighs and stomach began to arouser her sexual feelings.

Despite the hot sun she was covered in a fine sheen of warm moisture.

Shelbi used her hands to knead her breasts and her thumbs began to caress her soft red nipples. They responded and perked up into little cones poking out in the hot sun, enjoying the friction and the heat.

As she continued to caress her left breast, her palms slid over her nipple arousing it. Then her right hand slid down the moisture on her warm belly toward the red curly hair above her thighs. Her fingers caressed and tugged at it in a playful manner.

Her long middle finger began to rub and caress her hot vagina lips. She stroked first the right lip than the left swollen lip. Between the sun and the caressing of her stiff fingers plucking at her skin she could feel them getting engorged and sensitive.

Then she used two fingers pinching the lips together and feeling the slight sensation quiver through her legs.

Continuing to playfully pinch the lips between her fingers she slid her fingers up and down creating more urgency as she picked up the pace.

As the sensation continued to build in her thighs, she moved her fingers back and forth across her waiting clitoris. Eagerly awaiting her caresses, it grew stiffer as she rubbed it back and forth.

She could feel the wetness building between her thighs as her juices added to the moisture of the afternoon heat. Slowly she pried her vagina lip's part and rubbed one finger up and down the hot channel entrance. She shuddered slightly with a mini climax as she blurted out, "Oh that felt so good!"

She pulled her finger back and using two fingers to pick up the tempo of rubbing side to side across her stiff clitoris increasing the tension.

Her left-hand continue to caress her breasts and alternated rubbing her nipples that were tented and surrounded by pebbly areolas.

As her passion increased, she slowly inserted two eager fingers in her hot vagina. The wetness easily lubricated them as they slid in and out. Her fingers began to pick up the pace of moving in and out hitting the sides of her hot engorged lips. The sexy tension was rising in her channel as the fingers stimulated the sides.

Is a right-hand finger dipped in and out of her hot vagina as her left-hand took over command of her stiff and eager clitoris.

Three fingers of her left-hand picked up the pace of rubbing back and forth across her sensitive clitoris. She could feel the tension building. Finally, the tempo increased to a frantic pace. She buried her two fingers deep within her and focus solely on the sensation building between thighs.

As the climax finally came it shook her legs intensely, rolled up across her belly and made her nipples feel as if they were almost on fire.

She took her hands and cupped her breasts and felt the climax tremors in her legs slow down.

"I deserve that reward for all the hard work I put in getting here," Shelbi thought. For moment she considered a repeat performance but decided since she needed another swim in the lake to clean herself.

After coming out of the lake she laid face down on the rock to let the sun dry off her back. She slipped two fingers between her thighs thinking, *"Perhaps just one more time"*.

As she touched her waiting clitoris, she found that it was too sensitive right now and decided that she would not pleasure herself at this moment. Later, she would make time for one more session before she got to the end of the challenge.

Chapter 8 Strategy Paper Attack

Scanning the final grade sheet for the Wilderness Trak project posted on the screen in the grade lobby she smiled and said, "Yes! Top 5 percentile!"

The final grades were in on her trek assignment. They never gave exact grades merely percentiles. Shelbi had rated in the top 5 percentile of all people who had taken it this year.

She thought she had done well when she finished 16 hours ahead of the 18 days schedule timing.

As she had the debrief with the Lieutenant, she questioned her about cleaning your clothes the first time. She'd explain the situation and clarified questions she had.

The Lieutenant then asked her about the second time when she arrived at the water but there was a freak rainstorm for 48 hours. She had stonewashed all her clothes then created a lean-to structure and dried them with the heat of the fire. She wanted to know why she bothered.

Shelbi explained that microbes on alien planets could embed themselves in dirt. They could be picked up in a garment and lay dormant for months before they did their work of attacking the human. The Lieutenant made some notes but made no comments either for or against what Shelbi had done.

She now had passed the adventure trek, physics, biology, mathematics, chemistry and several other topics which allowed her to post her final strategy paper.

Each cadet needed to register their strategy paper to make sure that neither anyone in the second year or first year created a paper around the same nor even a similar topic. History had shown plagiarism created a problem. To avoid that the school had set up this regulation.

Shelbi had talked to Brendenn about the paper she wanted to do. He casually said, "If I could help, let me know."

As she walked back to her room. She felt pleased that her high grades confirmed she was excelling. She enjoyed the Warrior Academy. She enjoyed the learning and discovery that would lead her towards her ultimate career goal.

As she rounded the corner walking towards her room, she noticed someone striding purposely towards her.

The man about 6 foot 5 and physically well-built marched up to her and bluntly asked, "Shelbi MacPhadden?"

"Yes I am." Shelbi answered.

"It's time to pick another subject for your strategy paper."

"Why would I do that? Have you registered it? Is someone else registered it?" Shelbi knew the answers because she had researched before registering the paper. She knew that no one had actually written a paper on this topic for over 35 years.

He reached out his hand and put it on her left arm gripping it firmly. "MacPhadden, just change your paper to something else." The or else was understood even though he didn't voice it.

"I don't think I want to change the paper."

He increased the pressure on her left arm. Shelbi quickly folded her body into his torso. In surprise he loosened his grip slightly on her arm. Shelbi dropped to her right knee and swiftly brought her left leg around knocking him on his back. She countered the move by applying pressure to his neck.

As Shelbi finished her maneuver out of the corner of her eye, she saw movement. Continuing to pin her opponent down she glanced to her left. It was then she saw the two senior cadets.

The command was barked out. "Attention!"

Shelbi and her opponent leapt to their feet.

"Do we have a problem here cadets?" The tall blonde-haired senior cadet yelled.

"No sir!" Shelbi yelled.

"No sir," The cadet Shelbi had pinned sneered.

"Do we need to take this to the gym cadets?"

"No sir," They both yelled out.

Leaning into Shelbi's face the senior cadet yelled, "What's your name cadet?"

"Cadet MacPhadden sir."

Leaning into the other cadet's space he yelled the same question.

"Cadet Sloannay sir"

"I'm not writing up this time. But I have recorded both your names. If this is repeated, we will have a different discussion. Understood?"

"Sir yes sir." Shelbi immediately answered.

"Yea, okay," Cadet Sloannay mumbled.

"Yes, what cadet Sloannay!"

"Sir yes sir," Cadet Sloannay blurted out.

"Cadet MacPhadden on your way. Cadet Sloannay and I are going to continue our discussion."

Shelbi turned. As she did cadet Sloannay turned to her with a mask of fury on his face. "Change your subject," He spat.

Palming the door to her room open she stepped inside. She had no idea what else was going on. Nor did she care.

She thought, *"I should report this as an incident that gets physical."* However, when she thought about it her mind told her, *"It was just a little playful tussle nothing really to worry about."*

In a control room in another part of the building a video was being reviewed of the whole incident. The night duty Corporal and Lieutenant reviewed the video then laughed.

"It's time someone took that bully Sloannay down. The fact that it was a female will really irritate him."

The other security guard chimed in, "I doubt he'll reported to Calvinn. To be taken down by a little girl that's rich." He laughed out loud again.

"I wonder why Sloannay wants her to change her paper?" The lieutenant stated.

The Corporal. chimed in, "That bully is one of the protectors of Calvinn Devinn. They have some sort of family spat going on with Brendenn. Wonder how MacPhadden is involved? I wonder if we should report this?"

"No, they seem to work it out. The videos logged in and those involved in the incident have been noted. I don't think it warrants a special report."

The corporal had another thought.

"She did that very effectively. I like the move where she leaned into him before she executed her swing kick. Lulling him into a sense of surprise and then acting on it is excellent. You have to put this file away and note that cadet Shelbi MacPhadden should be considered for the warrior elite program."

Thus 3 things were set in motion that would change Shelbi's life forever.

Chapter 9 Stolen Paper Mystery

Shelbi was having one of those days. Brendenn had told her about some old documents that were actually in the secure library. Having registered her topic and gain security clearance she could go into the library and use it as research for her keystone strategy paper.

The commander had previously provided the insights that there would be documents in the library that would be important for her paper. Brendenn had explained his planet had loaned some documents for both safekeeping and use for student's research to the academy.

Shelbi arrived at the secure library and found the door was shut. The door screen noted that it was down for maintenance

Shelbi thought this was odd as she had registered and checked the maintenance schedule 48 hours before. It should be fine for at least 7 days before the next schedule maintenance check. She noted it would be available in 2 hours and went away and occupied herself.

Two hours later she arrived back and found the closed sign had disappeared. She keyed in her special security code set for her and moved into the room to look up the documents for her research. She was surprised to find the oldest document which was actually a scanned paper log, could not be found.

She thought maybe she had got the name wrong.

Shelbi keyed in a broader search and noted that the name of the two papers came up she was looking for. However, when she clicked to look at them neither paper could be found.

She found this odd and decided to follow up on it in the morning.

The morning, she arrived at the security library checkout center to discuss her challenge of finding the papers. It would start a chain of events that would unfold in several areas.

After the attendant did a quick search, he asked Shelbi to be patient. He was going off to check something.

Two-armed security guards came up and asked Shelbi to follow them.

They walked her down the corridor and into a very sterile gray room. A table and chair screwed to the floor was on one side of a table. On the other side were 2 chairs on wheels.

The security guard told Shelbi to sit in the chair that was screwed to the floor. As she sat down, she noticed a slight hum. She found that it was difficult to move around in a chair. She didn't think anything of it until two people came in and sat down in the chairs.

Behind them two security guards with helmets and shields on their faces walked in and stood beside each one of them.

"Shelbi MacPhadden, we understand that you went down to the secure library area last night. Tell us about that."

"I had arranged to go into the secure area to look at two research documents for my term paper. I arrived at my appointed time of 1 o'clock and the screen said that maintenance was being done and it was unavailable for 2 hours. I came back at 3 o'clock let myself in and sat down at the screen to find the documents. The first one could not be found. The second one could not be found. So, I did a broader scan and noted that the two documents were supposed to be there but I couldn't find them."

The second guard looked at her intensely and spoke up, "The security code shows you keyed in at 1 o'clock why did you do that?"

"Since I had registered the time, I wasn't sure if the maintenance meant that I couldn't go in or maintenance was being performed while I would be working. I keyed it in to see if the door would open allow me through. It didn't so I went away."

The shorter security guard flicked his fingers over a pad screen and the humming stopped in Shelbi's chair. She realized then that actually been doing a lie detector test to see if her heart rate rose or her blood pressure increased showing she was lying.

"What was that all about?" Shelbi asked.

"That's information we are not allowed to discuss with you cadet. Thank you for cooperation. You are free to go now"

Shelbi was a little miffed. It really seemed like overkill for documents she couldn't find.

She went to find Brendenn to explain her situation and see if they had any thoughts on how she could get the documents.

"Hello Brendenn I have a challenge with the research for my paper," Shelbi said.

Brendenn stood in front of her instinctively as his hands swung around and grabbed her buttocks. Shelbi smiled. She was used to this and after his explanation why he did she didn't really mind. It wasn't sexual it was just a reflex.

"This is all very strange Shelbi."

Shelbi frowned. "What strange is I'm just looking for two papers and they don't seem to be able to find them."

"It's actually a much bigger issue than that. The security check that stops you from going in to the library was not authorized. It does not appear anybody was actually in the library. It appears someone internally hacked into the library and either deleted or blocked those documents."

Shelbi thought it was time she shared with Brendenn when she had been confronted in the hallway about the research documents as she told the story Brendenn frowned.

"This is getting stranger and stranger. I know who that cadet is and who he is protecting."

"Back at my home planet there are several very powerful families. As you know my parents are the king and queen. Years ago, my great, great grandfather captured the existing king and took over the lineage that continues today. His brother split off and went into mining exploration and real estate. The two families never got along."

He paused to see if she had any comments. Why she didn't he moved on, "Historically they create the most problems for us. However, they are very powerful, have a lot of money, and continue to control mining not only on the home planet but on other planets in our galaxy. Since they have the exclusive rights to it bequeathed to them as part of the payoff not to create war against the king, they've used it and control it."

Shelbi crossed her arms over her chest. "While I don't know what to do really, I would like to see those papers as part of my research."

Brendenn seemed pensive. "Let me do some checking and see if I can come up with a solution."

If Shelbi had known what was about to transpire, she might've thought twice about accepting. If she had not accepted Brendenn's offer he would have died.

Chapter 10 Research Journey Home

Sabrinna pushed her chair back pulling out her tablet and began to type quickly. As she pushed back her elbow hit Brendenn in his side and caused him to look sharply at her.

She finished typing and putting her tablet on the table Brendenn smiled, "What was so important? And you know you jabbed in the side with your bony elbow!"

"Sorry about that," Sabrinna answered with a slight frown.

"I been working on the strategic war games case for over two weeks. And all of a sudden, I had two solutions to the strategic problems I've been trying to solve. I had to capture them immediately. I didn't want to forget them. It's really kind of strange. I have not been able to see head nor tail of the whole exercise and then I just felt a little warm and there were the two answers. Great now I can sleep better tonight."

"Do you often get as excited when you find a conclusion to some problem you're working on?" Shelbi asked.

"Well, it's always fun to find the answer or what you think is the answer. This was a little strange I'm never had such a complex solution come to me so quickly before. I guess I'm just getting better."

Shelbi began to think about all the changes that are incurred in the last couple of months. After taking Brendenn down in the hall and the secret discussion in the commander's office she had been accepted by the group as one of the few friends that weren't from Brendenn's planet.

For several subjects she had even join their study group. This is the third time that Sabrinna had noted she seemed to come to conclusions out of a cloud of data when the three of them sat close together.

Shelbi had explained to Brendenn her case for doing this strategy paper on this planets work. She also explained that she had tried to look for the old artifact material at the academy and they had strangely disappeared.

Brendenn had had a big smile when he came to see her the day before. "Shelbi we are going home for the spring celebration. How would you like to join us and do some research? My mother is in charge of the historical archive articles at the Royal Museum. I have approval for you to go to the private area to look at some of the old papers."

Shelbi was immediately excited, "Brendenn I can't thank you enough, that's wonderful. I was stalled on the paper and wasn't sure what to do. I didn't want to go back to the professor and ask him. When are you leaving?"

"The semester ends in three days so will be leaving in five days."

Shelbi had intended to go home on the break and perhaps have some rest and recreation. However, the opportunity to actually find some old log books and other materials that could support her major academic strategic paper was too hard to refuse.

"I will put the request for a study research session in to the commander tonight and see if I can be accommodated."

Now she was sitting quietly in her room. They had 8 days of travel time even with the migration onto the omni wavelength for 3 days of the trip.

Sabrinna approached Shelbi in the hall on day 5.

"Shelbi we are having a celebration session at the Blue Ozone club tomorrow. It's sort of a pre-celebration before we get back to the planet for the major spring celebration."

Shelbi had learned that this spring celebration was a huge ceremonial back on Brendenn's planet. Almost the entire planet celebrated the crops being put in the ground. The planet had never recorded a crop failure. They weren't sure exactly why they celebrated the ceremony just it was part of their long-standing traditions.

Shelbi thought for a moment. She was not a big drinker. She wasn't sure whether it was something in her chromosomes but after two drinks she could be the life of the party and out of control, not really something she enjoyed.

"Thank you very much Sabrinna but I think I'll take a pass. I'm not much for drinking parties."

"But Shelbi, is not just a drinking party. It's drinking and dancing and telling stories and just having fun. You will have a lot of fun if you go."

Shelbi thought about Brendenn being there. It would be kind of fun to see him relaxing and just spending time looking at his biceps as he lifted drinks.

"Okay Sabrinna, it's a deal."

"That's wonderful. And of course, you have a nice dress to wear, right?"

"Dress. No, I don't usually wear dresses. I do have my casual uniform."

"No, no, no, Shelbi let's see what you really look like in a dress. In fact, let's go shopping right now. You were going to go to dinner anyway. Let's take a detour see if we can find you a casual dress that you can wear to the party."

"Well, I'm not really sure about this. I'm not dress gal."

"Shelbi this is a casual fun time. You don't need the uniformed reminding you; you're a cadet. You want to get a dress and just have fun."

"Let's have dinner and will see about it afterwards." Shelbi thought this would be a good way to be able to put her off after dinner.

When they arrived at the cafeteria Brendenn, Dennek, and Channon the other two cadets for security had a large table with many people sitting around it. Sabrinna as usual took her spot just to the right hand of Brendenn. There was an empty chair beside her and she beckoned Shelbi to sit in it.

Near the end of the dinner Sabrinna mentioned to Brendenn that Shelbi had agreed to come to the Spring celebration at the Blue Ozone club.

Brendenn smiled and looked at Shelbi. "Wonderful I've always wanted to see you in a dress. Specially your spectacular legs!"

Shelbi was taken aback. She never thought about Brendenn wanting to see her legs. *This puts a whole new dimension on buying a dress,"* Shelbi thought.

"Well, my friend Brendenn, if I have a dress then you'll have to dance with me." Shelbi thought this was a good bet she'd heard the Brendenn was not a keen dancer. She was sure this would put them off and she could avoid the dress.

"Shelbi MacPhadden I would be pleased to have a dance with you." Sabrinna was now the one taken aback knowing how Brendenn's was not fond of dancing.

"Really, dance with me?" Shelbi tentatively commented.

Brendenn leaned across Sabrinna to get closer to Shelbi and quietly said, "Shelbi I've always wanted to make amends for the way I treated you. And I know where you come from dancing is an important social activity. I would love to do it."

After dinner Shelbi and Sabrinna went off to the ships Store Lane. They visited several stores. In each one Shelbi tried on several dresses. Then she found one that she was happy with. It was a light blue and showed off her red hair amazingly. It had little short sleeves and came down to about an inch above her knee. The slight flare the skirt had would be enjoyable and comfortable to sit in. It would also make dancing easy.

The next night Shelbi showed up at the Blue Ozone club determined to have fun and limit her drinking so she wasn't out of control.

As she moved up to the table that Brendenn and his crew were sitting around she noticed all the chairs were full except one beside Sabrinna which was leaning against the table. She assumed that she was late and therefore there probably wasn't a seat at the table. As she approached them Sabrinna jumped up "Shelbi, Shelbi I had been saving this chair for you. Come sit by me."

Nobody else seemed to notice Sabrinna's outburst so although Shelbi felt a little awkward, she walked around the table, pulled the chair back and sat down. Just as she sat down the hostess put down a tray of slim green tube glass drinks.

"Shelbi you are just in time. We are going to toast the King and Queen with our special spring drink," Sabrinna mentioned as she passed one to Shelbi.

"It's not really strong, is it? You know we had the talk about how well I do if I drink too much," Shelbi said.

"Shelbi this is our national drink it's not strong at all."

Brendenn stood up and they all stood up. He said something in his native language which he then repeated in English. "To the health, wealth and safety of our Queen." They all raised their drinks and Shelbi noted everybody else took it as a shot.

As she sat down, she felt the liquor burned down her throat into her belly. At the same time, she realized that this was a strong high proof liquor. What they and their larger bodies didn't think was very high proof, hit her as a nondrinker.

Seconds later another tray was there and Brendenn announced they were going to drink to the success of the spring celebration.

Shelbi was now little worried she knew if she had two of these, she could get out of control so she thought, *"I'll think I will only drink part of it."*

Brendenn made his speech in his native language than English and everybody's shot back their drinks. Shelbi shot half of hers then sat down. Immediately several people began to chant, "Shelbi, Shelbi," Sabrinna whispered in her ear, "You need to finish the drink."

Shelbi shot the rest of it down and sat there with a nice warm buzz. Having finished the drink, the buzz was even larger and she felt compelled to dance with Brendenn now!

She got out of her chair grab Brendenn's arm and said, "Let's dance my friend."

Brendenn got out of his chair, "Absolutely Shelbi." And he took her out onto the dance floor.

As they arrived the music shifted from one that had been energetic and having people move quickly to a slow sexy romantic dance.

Brendenn tucked his arm around Shelbi in the small of her back and pulled her into his body. Her breasts touched his rock-hard chest and as she reached up her left-hand to take his right hand to dance. She could feel the heat moving down her body.

Her nipples began to harden and she began to think about what he might be like to make love too.

She had heard some of the tales from some of the other ladies that he was a gentle lover. At the same time, he made sure they were satisfied before he took his pleasure.

Shelbi began thinking of how he might satisfy her if they ever had the opportunity. She began to imagine his fingers trailing down her back, raising goosebumps on her ivory flesh.

She shook her head. She had to stay focused on the dancing so she didn't stumble and make a fool of herself.

Brendenn meanwhile was having a reaction that he hadn't expected.

"I was really glad she asked me to dance," he thought. *"It seems like a good idea to pull her into my chest. But the softness of her breasts against my chest is giving a reaction I hadn't expected. This small of her back against my hand just creating some heat up my arm. And the fragrant smell coming off her beautiful red hair is absolutely amazing."*

As they danced and she shifted her weight into his body he began to think about her beautiful legs showing below her dress as she walked up to the table.

He knew she had her curvy hip based on the military uniform she wore. But he wasn't prepared for the beautiful shapely legs he saw.

As they danced, he had the urge to run his hands over those bare legs. He wondered what it would be like to run his fingers along the outside of her hips and then down the back of her legs. He wondered if it would give her goosebumps or is, she one of those ladies it didn't like being touched.

As they continue to dance Shelbi murmured to him, "Hold me tight my Prince."

Brendenn was startled at her comment. Shelbi shifted her weight again and had a rhythm going back and forth. She was rubbing her breasts across his chest and her hand had crept up in the hair at the back of his neck. She was stroking the back of his neck and he could feel his manhood reacting.

The music finished and Brendenn went to walk off the dance floor but Shelbi stopped him.

"What one dance. That's not fair as a duty call. I want to have another one."

Timing is everything and the music started another romantic slow dance song.

Shelbi immediately cuddled into Brendenn's body. *"My gosh the softness of her body and those wonderful breasts. I wonder what it would be like to kiss her nipples caressing them with my lips."*

Shelbi by now was slightly out of control. Her mind was wandering as her hand slid down his broad back across his buttocks to his hip. She then reached up both arms and caressed the softness behind his neck. To do that she was on her toes.

"My gosh she's on her toes. Those beautiful legs will be stretched. It would be wonderful to see what she looks like."

Just at that moment they dance past a set of mirrors that been set up to shine light around. Brendenn slow down and just rocked back and forth. Shelbi thought that was wonderful and just leaned into him more. What Brendenn was really doing is glancing at the mirror and studying those beautiful legs of Shelbi stretched on her toes.

He could stand to know more and slipped his hands under her arms lifted her up and nuzzled into her neck. The he gave her a kiss after kiss after kiss. Shelbi circled his neck and nuzzled his neck then began to kiss him.

Just as they were about to zone out someone accidentally danced into them.

Startled Brendenn put Shelbi down and backed off a little.

Sabrinna was the one who had danced into them looking at them she quietly said, "Get a room, get off the dance floor."

Shelbi immediately felt the hot flush roll over her face. She was embarrassed and realize she'd been making a spectacle. At the moment though it didn't seem to really matter.

Brendenn also realized he may have been taking advantage of Shelbi and her situation. But she had returned his kiss. This was something that he had dreamt about.

Brendenn took Shelbi back to the table and as she sat down. Another round of green slim drinks had been set up on the table. Shelbi reached out and grabbed one and saluted Brendenn. "To the second-best warrior next to me here" then shot the green liquor back.

Brendenn thought, *"I'm not sure she's a real drinker. She goes from anymore I will be carrying her back to her room never mine walking her back.*

Sabrinna arrived back at the table and said to Shelbi that she had to visit the ladies' room. Shelbi stood up a little unsteady on her feet and shook her head. "Wonderful I will come with you"

As they walked away slowly Brendenn gazed at Shelbi's beautiful legs and his mind began to wander. He wondered what it would be like slipped the blue dress off her. To have her down on her bare back with the redhaired splayed across a pillow. He started to imagine kissing up the inside of her leg and what he would do if he got all the way to the middle of her thighs.

When Shelbi came back to the table, she again grabbed Brendenn and said, "Let's dance."

Brendenn had spent a little too much time thinking about Shelbi and realized that his hardness would show at the front of his pants when he moved to dance. However, with a few drinks he had he just didn't care.

Out on the dance floor it was more energetic number then they'd had before. Shelbi showed that she really was a good dancer. "I can't believe how great a dance you are. You should've told me before," Brendenn said.

Shelbi looked at him, "But I thought you didn't like to dance."

"I'm not keen on dancing because usually when I dance with someone it then gets reported that I now have girlfriend. Next, they say we are getting married. Which means there's a new Queen. It just gets all carried away. I prefer not to do things in public."

"Well, I'm not a big dancer either but I am really enjoying myself tonight." With that Shelbi twirled off started dancing around him. Brendenn saw the skirt swirl and saw more of her legs. This created additional tension. Not only was he now hard but really warm and he unbuttoned the top two buttons of his shirt.

Shelbi was also dancing energetically and felt warm. But she thought taking off her dress was probably not a good idea. The more she looked at Brendenn the more she saw how happy he was to be dancing with her. She began to fantasize about what it would feel like to caress her fingers on that hardness showing up the front of his pants.

The music changed again to a soft romantic number Shelbi almost flung herself at Brendenn. She slipped her arms round his neck and slowly pushed against his hardness.

Brendenn was now trying to decide what to do. He wouldn't be able to dance very long with her rubbing against him but he couldn't stop.

She slipped in your hand inside his shirt and flicked his nipple little bit. He caressed her hand and took it out.

"This is definitely not the place to do that Shelbi."

"But you smell so good. You feel so good. And I want more."

Brendenn began to realize that Shelbi had had just about enough to drink. Her other hand wandered the other side of his chest and her fingers travelled over the plains of his breast. She gently caressed his nipple then took her hand out inside put her cheek against his bare belly. Her tongue licks the salty moisture. Brendenn picked her up and walked off the dance floor.

He knew this had gone quite far enough. He was almost at the point of no return himself. If Shelbi kept this up, he really would have her over in the corner of the room.

Before he got back to the table Sabrinna was up beside him.

"You do know you have your hand almost up her dress." Sabrinna said as she looked sharply at Brendenn.

At that moment Brendenn realized he had enough to drink too. Yes, when he picked Shelbi up his hand it slid down her leg almost to her frilly yellow panties. Shelbi sat down in the chair and Sabrinna said, "Shelbi perhaps it's time to go."

"Not yet I think I still have one more drink in me and at least another half hour dancing with Brendenn"

Once again, she showed she was faster than the group as her hand rushed out grasping one of the tall green drinks and chugging it before anybody could think.

Brendenn who metabolize liquor very quickly realize that it was better to get Shelbi back to her room. She might regret what was going on in the morning and he really didn't want to set back their relationship.

He looked at Sabrinna, "I'll take her back to her room now not to worry."

Brendenn needn't have worried because Shelbi was one of those people who when she drank too much could not remember what had happened. Beyond the first dance and hoping they had a second, she wouldn't remember anything in the morning.

Brendenn carried Shelbi through the ship back to her room. Sabrinna had given him her purse to carry after pulling out the data card that would allow entry into her room.

Shelbi had snuggled into his arms as they walked along and was nearly asleep by the time they got to her room.

He put her on her feet, touch the data card to the panel and the door opened.

She turned around and gazed at him, "Is this your room or mine?"

"It's your room."

"I'd rather it your room." Brendenn realized this was one of those conversations that people have when they've had too much to drink that doesn't go anywhere. He picked her up again and stepped into her room walking over to her bed.

As he later down on her bed her dress rocked up and showed most of her legs. Being the gentleman, he simply covered her up and went back to get Sabrinna.

When they met the next morning, Shelbi started off by apologizing. "Brendenn I'm so sorry I know we had at least one dance and I think two together but after that I don't really remember what happened. Sabrinna says you carry me back to my room. I really appreciate that."

Brendenn felt saying nothing was the best course of action at this point

Shelbi looked at him and her face began coloring, "I have to ask though did you take my dress off? Did we do anything else?"

"I never take advantage of ladies who have had a little too much to drink. Or sleeping ladies. And no, I didn't take your dress off. I went back and got Sabrinna and she helped you out of your dress."

At this point Shelbi did not know what else to say other than, "Thank you". She walked calmly off reminding yourself not to drink the slim green drinks ever again.

Brendenn on the other hand watched her walk away and just saw the flashes of her bare legs below her dress as they danced together the night before. He realized he wanted more than just a casual look or nuzzled kisses.

Chapter 11 Death Surrounding the Prince

Shelbi pace the floor covering the distance between her desk and the door of her room for the 156 time. Yes, she had counted them. She could stand it no longer. It'd been 5 days since Brendenn had been taken away on the emergency med's stretcher. She had gone to the hospital twice and each time turned away since she wasn't family.

Then the message from Brendenn's mother. Please come and see me now! Shelbi grabbed her key fobs and her cadet jacket and walk swiftly out to her electric car. She was going to see Brendenn's mother and hopefully get to help her friend and fellow cadet.

When she arrived at the magnificent house she drove straight to the front door. Jumping out of her car she ran up the red granite stairs and press the front door bell. Out of the corner of her eye she saw the security camera and turn. She turned her face towards it smiling. "Shelbi MacPhadden requesting to talk to Mrs. Miriam Southernn." Shelbi spoke to the camera.

Almost immediately the door opened and a beautiful middle-age woman stood before her. "Hello Shelbi it's good of you to come so fast," Miriam said.

"I just can't stand it any longer I really need to see Brendenn!" Shelbi stated emphatically.

She stared at her for a moment. "Please stepped in Shelbi."

"Do you mind if I give you a hug my dear?"

"Not at all ma'am."

As Miriam gave Shelbi the hug, she thought she felt something. Her son had said Shelbi was special but not in a girlfriend sort of way. She was special in some way he hadn't figured out.

Looking at Shelbi and feeling that surge of energy she made up her mind. "We tried just about everything else let's see what happens if you see him".

When they arrived at the hospital, they rode the elevator up to the 23rd high security floor. As they stepped out of the elevator doors, they were immediately surrounded by three heavily armed guards. One step back and motion for Miriam to go forward but reached out a hand to stop Shelbi.

"She's a family friend and with me as his mother. It is imperative that the two of us go and see him now," Miriam spoke with authority.

"Fine but we need to have a palm scan, a retinal scan, and blood type before she moves in a further," Spoke the taller of the three guards.

"I will gladly do that," Shelbi said.

She moved over to the Guards security station and stared into the retinal scan device as it locked onto her to eyes. At the same time, she put her hands down for the palm scans and felt the perk in both palms as blood was drawn to get her DNA sample.

The senior guard saluted Shelbi. "Excuse me Cadet MacPhadden I didn't know. You have already had high security clearance. I believe you were here earlier in the week and we did not let you in. Sorry about that."

"I understand. Security of Brendenn is paramount and I'd rather you be over cautious," Shelbi said.

Together Miriam and Shelbi walked down the short corridor to Brendenn's med suite. One quarter of the entire floor was taken up with the secure section. Outside of his room was the nurse's station with several monitors and 3 nurses watching them. Bella the brunette blue-eyed nurse turned to Shelbi and Miriam.

"No change in Brendenn today ma'am," she said solemnly.

Shelbi slid off her jacket and walk forward to the hand scanner. Palming the security pad, the doors slid back and she walked into the room where Brendenn lay still. For 5 days he had laid there in a coma not moving. Not doing anything. His 24 body sensors showing he was in hibernation.

Shelbi walked over and grasped his right hand. She leaned down and whispered in his ear.

"This is another fine mess. It's time you stop playing around and got up to get back to work. Besides you owe me a dance."

Shelbi a barely get out the words and the door sprang back. Both Miriam and the nurse ran into the room.

"What exactly did you do!" The nurse questioned.

"I merely took his hand and told him to stop lazing around."

"When you did that 3 of the 24 brain waves, we are monitoring had a brief movement. Two have stayed slightly elevated. I'm going to call Dr. Enos the neurosurgeon immediately. Please don't let go of his hand," The nurse warned.

Moments later the neurosurgeon ran up to the monitoring station. The nurse had gone back to the monitor and showed him what she believed was movement of the 3 brain waves.

"I'm not sure if that's real movement are not," Dr. Enos said.

"I have a question for you cadet Shelbi. How close are you to Brendenn? By that I mean are you just friends, battle companions or have you been more intimate with them?"

"Sir if you're asking have, I made love with Brendenn the answer is no. We are just battle companions," Shelbi said slightly embarrassed.

"I want you to go back in and take his hand and put your cheek next to his. You can whisper in his ear or not. I'm interested in what happens physically if you touch him in a comforting way."

Shelbi when into the room taking Brendenn's hand again and bent down and rubbed her right cheek against his right cheek. His stubble felt itchy. Shelbi stayed there cheek to cheek, for a few minutes then stood up, and walked back out to the monitors.

"That was very interesting, I think three of the brain waves seen to do something. You have a connection that we need to explore. It's almost as if he's talking to himself back and forth," Dr. Enos said.

Miriam and Dr. Enos went off to have a conversation in a private room in the med suite. Shelbi wasn't part of it and had no idea what they were talking about.

When they emerged from the room Miriam asked Shelbi would she please join her. Shelbi entered the room the door closed and Miriam turned to her.

"Shelbi you have something that may help my son. Are you willing to do almost anything to see if we can get Brendenn out of this terrifying hibernation?"

"Ma'am, I would do anything to get my friend back," Shelbi said forcefully.

Miriam looks Shelbi straight in the eye and took a deep breath in and let a sigh.

"The doctor feels strongly that if you can get more intimate with him it may stimulated him to come back to us."

Shelbi remained silent waiting for Miriam to continue.

"The doctor would like you to consider sleeping with my son,"

Shelbi was slightly taken aback. However, while she had not slept with him before she was willing to try anything to wake him up.

"Yes, ma'am I'd be glad to do whatever it takes. If sleeping with your son is what it takes, I will do it."

Miriam stood up and took Shelbi by the hand and started to walk out of the room. As she passed the nurses station she said, "Belle, we will be back in several hours."

Chapter 12 Secret Before Sleeping with the Prince

Shelbi wasn't sure where they were going but followed Miriam instinctively.

They got into Miriam's electric car. Her fingers flew over the screen as she programmed it too self-drive. When the car started to move, she turned to Shelbi.

"I am taking you to Brendenn's Great Grand Nann. I'm not sure why I just have an instinct that you need to talk to her. She has more wisdom than my mother and me put together. She's old and even with regeneration prefers not to leave her home for any great distance or drive. I'm sorry I should've asked you before we started this. Is this a challenge?"

"Ma'am, trusting our instincts is what is kept Brendenn and myself alive or at least uninjured in some of the battles the we have fought already. Instinct is what can be the difference between success and failure in any action or plan."

"I should tell you that Gran Nann Rebecca has instincts built in that hearken back to the original colonists. She often does or says things that are almost spooky. I'm simply warning you so you won't be too surprised that some of the things she may say or do." Miriam said with love in her voice.

As they arrived at the palatial grounds of the Grand Nann's home Shelbi was again struck by the wealth of the family and their position on the planet. She had always just thought of Brendenn at first as pain in the ass, then adversary and now a friend. When she realized he was royalty and someday would rule half the planet she wasn't quite sure what to make of it.

As the car rolled up to the red wood front door Shelbi saw that it was open and an older woman was standing in the doorway. The car doors opened and they both got out. Miriam glanced up at the older woman, "Hello Rebecca I think we need to talk to you."

As they walked up the red stone stairs Rebecca put out her hand. "Hello Cadet Shelbi it's a pleasure to see you."

Shelbi hesitated for a moment wondering how she knew who she was since they had never met.

"Brendenn has told me about you and some of the adventure stories you've already had. That's why I knew who you were," Rebecca's said.

They walked into the sitting room and Shelbi noted that pot of tea and some small sandwiches were on the table.

"I had a call from Dr. Enos about what he was thinking for my Brendenn. I thought you needed to eat before you spent the night sleeping with Brendenn," said Rebecca with warmth.

"Now, now, I'm an elderly woman I know when two people have a thing for one another in this modern day and age. Yes, I know you are going to get naked together. I have a sense that may be just what we need to unlock this mystery."

Shelbi almost chocked at the words the Great Grand Nann spoke.

Shelbi was finishing her tea and sandwiches as the Grand Nann stood up and step towards her. "I'd like to hug you, Shelbi," she said.

Shelbi stood up and walked over to the woman noting they were about the same height. Shelbi put her arms around her and began to hug her. While she looked frail, she was strong and pulled Shelbi into her and held onto her tightly. She kept holding on and Shelbi wasn't sure when to let go.

When she stepped back the Gran Nann put her right hand to her chest.

"Are you all right Rebecca?" Miriam said.

"She has the energy. She has something I haven't felt for many, many years."

"Miriam you were right. The blood work we did on Shelbi after the dinner to make sure she had not been poisoned, showed some odd DNA and equally interesting chromosome structure we had not seen for many centuries. I don't know why but somewhere in her background is an ancestor who had the gift. It's imperative she wear my old meteor pendant."

Brendenn's mother looked very surprised. In all the years she had known Rebecca, she had never known her to take the pendant off.

The Gran Nann took the pendant off her neck and slipped it out of the front of her tunic.

"Shelbi please take your jacket off," Miriam said.

Gran Nann walked over and put the pendant around Shelbi sliding it over her hair. Shelbi pulled the front of her shirt out and dropped it down her front. It rested just in between her breasts and felt warm. Then it started to feel prickly almost like little shocks were coming off it. Shelbi stepped back.

"It is commonly called a tremble stone. It reacts to certain people. What is it doing to you?" Gran Nann asked.

Shelbi staggered back and was holding onto the arm of the chair. "When you first put on nothing. Now it feels warm and prickly. Like little shocks running over my breasts."

Gran Nann sucked in her breath. "That is simply amazing. I haven't heard of that except in legends."

Shelbi broken out in a fine sweat on her forehead and upper lip. Finally, she sat down on a nearby chair and took several deep breaths.

"It seems to calm down but still fills warm against my skin."

"The pendant is extremely old. My Great Grand Nann gave it to me. It's believed to stretch back almost to the golden era of our people. As you know the legend has it there are 3 kinds of people that make up the power energy triangle. One is someone who receives the energy. One is someone who channels the energy. One is someone who translates what the energy produces. It's been years since we found three people to form a triangle. I'm not sure if you're one of them but they're certainly been a reaction here that I haven't seen over 100 years. You may be a receiver."

"You must make sure you wear it tonight and if possible, lie bare chested with my great-grandson."

This intimate talk was much different from what Shelbi experience when she was with her family. She found it interesting and soothing all of the same time. As Rebecca talks some more about Brendenn the soothing nature of her words seems to fold over and make her seem calm. She realized it was the effect of the pendant.

When they arrived back at the medical center Shelbi quickly went through the scans to enter. The journey, dinner and all the events that transpired had taken several hours and it was now after 10 o'clock at night.

"Shelbi you should be aware that we have monitors and recording at all times of Brendenn. We are looking for any motion. We also have the 24 scan monitors. Should he make any movement we would note that on our alert," Dr. Enos explained.

Shelbi thought about that and then decided it really didn't matter. Yes, they would see her nude getting into bed with Brendenn but if by the morning if he had moved or increased any of his brain waves it would be worth it.

She thought it was important that the doctor knew she was wearing a tremble stone from the Great

Grand Nann. When she told him he seemed very surprised.

"I'm one of those doctors that's not sure about all these old legends. At the same time, I always believed there some truth in what's going on with them. If the Gran Nann gave that to you then please wear it. I should tell you that it may have some reaction while you wear it. Legend has it that the stones bond with people. You may feel heat. That's a good thing."

Shelbi thought for a moment and then asked the question, "Would there be any other sensations or prickly feelings?"

The doctor's head snapped around and he looked at Shelbi with his eyes even wider open.

"Why would you ask that? Again, it's only legend the prickly feeling is deep bonding and usually when it's going to the person who can channel energy."

Shelbi didn't answer but strode up to Brendenn's room putting her palm on the security scan. The door opened. She went inside and took off her clothes. She hung them up on the closet. Standing in her blue lacy bra and matching lacy panties she remembered the Gran Nann suggesting she be bare breasted for her to better bonded with him. She stripped off the bra and walked to the bed.

Shelbi got up on the steps and pulled his cover back. They had stripped the clothing off him when they heard Shelbi was going to sleep with him.

She lay down beside his naked body and threw her right leg over his right leg. She adjusted slightly so she wasn't crushing his manhood. She then laid her bare breasts touching his beautiful chest. She put her hands over her chest. It will be difficult to sleep but she had to make the best of it.

The earpiece they had given her came alive with the whisper voice of the young nurse. "Eight of the 24 wavelengths are showing signs of movement."

Shelbi felt odd lying beside the inert figure of Brendenn. But realize that she was trying to bring them out of the coma and anything that was required should be tried.

She began to run her fingers up and down his body like a lover's caress. At the same time, she began to hum a lullaby her mother used to sing to her when she wasn't feeling well.

Again, the whisper in her ear, "11 of 24"

As she continued to caress him, she felt slightly erotic. She knew it was crazy, but she was actually starting to get warm between her thighs. She knew that some wetness was pooling their and she felt awkward.

At the same time, she felt him getting warmer and thought they were all good signs.

Again, the whisper in her ear, "18 of 24. With 7 at 80%."

She moved up slightly on his body pressing her breasts to his chest. She was straddling his leg and resisted the urge to rub up and down on his fine silky skin.

Then the magic whisper that they'd all been waiting for, "24 of 24 moving".

Shelbi kept up her caresses and started to softly kiss cheek. She ran her fingers lightly over his lips.

She began to kiss across his cheek and down his neck. He seemed to take a big sigh.

Shelbi notice that the pendant was very warm. The prickly feeling across her breasts increased right to her nipples.

And she noticed that his right arm was moving as his hand was trailing his fingertips over her skin. He got to her backside and cupped her bottom. Then he ran his fingers back down her part of her leg and up again.

He seemed to turn his head ever so slightly as he ran his fingers up the smooth skin of her back.

She continued to run her hands up and down his chest then the side of his hip. Kissing him gently. He turned his head to Shelbi.

"It took you long enough to get here. I have been waiting all night," Brendenn whispered.

The whisper voice in her ear said, "Don't mention it, don't mention time."

She noticed now that his manhood had risen and was pressing against the side of her leg. It had been encased in the event that he urinated. Now it was like wearing a condom given how hard and stiff he was.

Shelbi decided to continue pressing and kissing him. With the right hand she started to play with his left nipple caressing it and running her palm around it. He had closed his eyes but was sighing heavily and his hand was roaming up-and-down her back and occasionally cupping the warm cheeks of her backside.

Suddenly he grabbed her hips and pulled her on top of himself. She was now straddling him like a jockey on a horse. His manhood tip was pressing the cloth of her panties pressing her glistening vagina lips. She had no idea where this was going but the erotic sensual nature was taking over and she just didn't care.

His hands were running up and down her back and across her legs as she continued to kiss his cheeks and his neck.

The pendant around her neck was hot but seemed to settle into his chest in a groove between her breasts. His hands roamed over her shoulders and down to the breasts and started to flick her erect pink nipples.

His hands went back to the side of her thighs and picked her up, pulled her panties aside, and slowly impaled the folds of her pulsating vagina on his stiff manhood. The sudden shock of him entering her and sliding slowly up her hot channel took her breath away.

Once he impaled her, he seemed to just lie there holding her tightly against his body.

Shelbi was glad she had taken the yellow pill to allow her vagina to stretch and accept Brendenn's large member as it slide inside her.

Minutes went by. Then his hands clutched her thighs and started to move her along with the rhythm of his thighs. He began to slide up and down the wetness of her vagina. When he had nearly pulled completely out of her. He played slightly at the mouth of her engorged vagina lips. Then plunged back into her slick warmth.

She grabbed onto his shoulders and rode him with all the passion she now felt.

The covers fall away and she was sure everyone could see their naked lustful movements on the monitor. Overtaken with the whole sensation she could not stop herself.

His rhythm picked up as he forced her down onto his manhood and plunged deep within her. Then pulled her up, to plunge again and again.

She came first. Vagina walls clutching his immense manhood demanding its essence, clutching and not letting it loose.

Her legs were quivering as the strong climax rode all over her body. For one brief moment she felt the pendant shooting sensations across her breasts and down to her copper triangle.

At last, he held her tightly as his manhood juices exploded inside her. Despite the sheath like condom Shelbi could still feel the heat. She had only imagined the wonderful sensation of him being naked in her.

She slid off to one side and said, "Brendenn that was absolutely amazing. The energy that you provide for me is indescribable."

Shelbi pulled the covers over their bottom half of their naked bodies and began to talk to Brendenn.

She sat up on her elbow and ran her hand over the fine sheen of sweat on his chest. He opened his eyes and looked at her.

"I'm in a hospital." Brendenn exclaimed. "What am I doing here, what is all this?"

Shelbi kissed him on the lips knowing he'd shut his eyes when she did that. She waited for the voice in the ear to tell her what to do next. It did not fail her.

"I'd like to come in and explained to him what's going on. It's important that you state just where you are. I want him to stay connected to you because there's some rhythm going on between the two of you, I can't explain. We'll talk about it another time." Dr. Enos said.

The door slid open to the room and Dr. Enos walked in not wearing his white lab coat but casual blue shirt and soft brown slacks. "Hello Brendenn."

"Hello Tony," said Brendenn.

"Yes, you are in my hospital. We'll talk about this in the morning right now I'd like you to try to go back to sleep. Shelbi will stay with you. Right now, that's the best thing you can do."

With that Tony turned around and walked out. Shelbi snuggled up against him a little embarrassed at the juices running down her leg and across his. He kissed her lightly on the forehead.

"Yes, all of a sudden I feel sleepy," Brendenn said.

Shelbi notice the pendant had gone cool and seemed to be resonating with the fact they had to sleep.

He ran his left hand up and down her naked side several times. And he rested his right hand on her left bottom cheek. He seemed content and then softly slipped into a slumber.

Shelbi snuggled up and waited till she heard the whisper voice in their ear, "Slumber level, still 24 of 24 OK." she then slid little off the side rather than having him bare all her weight.

In the morning, she would talk to him along with the doctor about all that had transpired. The good news was her Brendenn was back.

She doesn't think she had to stay with him since he was out of the coma. She asked Dr. Enos and he felt it was safe for her to leave him. She slipped out of the covers and gathering up her clothes. Then she stepped into in the bathroom to have a quick shower.

As she exited the door she stopped by Belle.

"Yes, he's doing fine. He's in really deep sleep but not slipped back into a coma level."

As Shelbi turned around Dr. Enos was there.

"Shelbi in the morning he probably won't remember this entire incident. While he appeared to be totally conscious and functioning, I don't believe he was. Yes, he's out of his coma. I don't believe he's really aware of what went on. We call it, coma amnesia. People often come out of comas but don't remember what transpires for several days. Since he's been deep for a long time, I don't believe he will remember anything of tonight"

"So, you're saying he may not remember us making love."

"Absolutely correct. In fact, given how he was functioning I would almost guarantee he will not remember it. It's part of the mind preparing itself. It enjoys the good things but is still working on the bad things."

Shelbi would later learn the Brendenn had no memory of that night. He did remember coming out of the coma and seeing Shelbi's face but that's all. The memory of his love making was hers to cherish alone.

Chapter 13 Poisoner Uncovered

While Brendenn and Shelbi were in the throes of their sensual exploration Sabrinna sat outside his med room. The three protector companions had cycled through every 8 hours since Brendenn came to the hospital. They felt it important to be there should he wake up and to guard him from anything else that might happen.

Suddenly, Sabrinna saw the party where the prince was stricken. The situation unraveled as a vision in her head.

She was standing beside Brendenn talking to him about how glad she was to be home. Then she noticed his eyes looking over her shoulder and a smile crossed his lips. He turned and saw Shelbi and that wonderful blue dress she wore walking towards him.

"She really has wonderful legs," Brendenn quietly murmured.

Shelbi had begun talking to Brendenn about how excited she was to be at this Royal reception.

Next, she saw the waiter working his way through the crowd of with a drink on a serving platter. Several people reached out to pick it up and he seemed to fend them off and keep moving. He came up to Shelbi and offered her the drink as she didn't have one.

As she went to reach for it, he stepped back and used a cloth to wipe the moisture off the edges.

Brendenn had his glass in his left hand and put it down on the plate picked up the glass and quickly took his usual manly gulp.

Seconds later he fell to his knees as the glass fell to the ground.

With the prince on the floor most people didn't notice what was happening, but Sabrinna could see it clearly in her vision.

Out of the corner of her eye she saw the waiter pick up the glass fold the cloth around it and quietly walk out through the garden doors.

With all the commotion with Brendenn stricken and soft green foam flowing from his mouth nobody thought to check out what the waiter was doing.

Sabrinna replayed the scene several times in her mind. It was clear the waiter had brought the drink for

Shelbi. She realized with startling clarity the poison had been meant to kill Shelbi. The Prince having internal nano medibots and being much larger had not been killed by the drink, just placed in a coma.

She wasn't sure why she could see it so clear now but she knew the action to be taken was to get the security footage and track down the waiter.

If she had realized why she had the vision things and what part Shelbi had in them it would have saved lives and Brendenn would not have been injured so severally later.

Chapter 14 Mystical Pendent Discovery

Shelbi was very excited when the invitation came from the Great Grand Nann for an afternoon tea.

She thought it was strange when Brendenn message her that it was really important to him that she come to the tea. She hadn't realized he would be there.

As she drove up the pathway to the magnificent home her mind slipped back to the first time she'd been here in the middle of the night. Brendenn's mother had brought her here as part of the emergency surrounding Brendenn's coma illness. The Great Grand Nann had given her the pendant she still wore.

Perhaps the Great Grand Nann wanted it back.

She walked into the sunlit atrium at the back of the house and was taken aback. The Great Grand Nann was there with both Brendenn and Sabrinna.

"Welcome Shelbi it's so nice to see you again," The Great Grand Nann said with a smile.

"The honour is mine Great Grand Nann." Shelbi bowed as she said the formal greeting.

"Come sit down beside me and I'll pour you some tea," Then the Great Grand Nann picked up the teapot and poured a cup for all four of them.

"Shelbi, Brendenn, and Sabrinna it's time we brought all the loose threads together so you can see exactly what is unfolding."

All three of them paused with their tea cups in the air. They were surprised at the statement and realized this was more than just a social afternoon tea.

"I will do most of the talking," the Great Grand Nann said. "Some of the things I have to say may sound outrages, unbelievable, perhaps like a funny story from an old lady. However, I assure you most of what you are going to hear is not just a fable."

Brendenn placed his cup on the table and sat back in the chair. Sabrinna took a long sip of the beautiful green tea. Shelbi sip her black tea twice then put the cup down. They all waited for the Great Grand Nann to settle back with her teacup in her hand and begin talking.

"The fable goes that we were once a great warrior nation of a great Empire. We seem to have the ability to take all aliens on. No matter how tough the battle we always seem to end up victorious even if we lost a few skirmishes. No one understood how we could do it again and again."

She paused and waited to see if there is any reaction or questions. All three seem focused and waiting.

"The fable goes there was an energy and special people that created the ability for us to win. The answer is that's true. I'm going to tell you how my husband explained it to me. I'm going to help you understand how it works and why the three of you are so important."

She took a sip of her tea and continued, "The reality is it's a triangle. At the one corner is a person who can receive, collect and absorbs the energy swirling through the universe called a Gatherer. At one corner is the person who focuses the gathered energy called a Channeler. At the third corner is a person who the energy comes to and they create a vision beyond what others can see in the universe called a Translator. I know this because my husband did research for years trying to find out how to identify the triangle people. They key he looked for was the energy person to gather and focus the energy."

The Great Grand Nann stopped talking and took another sip of her tea. Seeing there were no questions she continued.

"The answer is hanging around Shelbi's neck. That piece of stone was supposed to come from a meteor that the first settlers brought to this planet. That stone has ability to help gather the energy with the energy person of the triangle. For whatever reason Shelbi is that person. That explains your role Brendenn. Shelbi absorbs the energy and sends it to you. You channel the flow. Without you it simply sits swirling around Shelbi. With you it begins to move and flow. Your attraction to Shelbi and the feeling of energy is exactly what happened. It was very slight because she didn't have the stone. Now she has the stone you're getting at the more." She paused to let these insights sink in.

Looking at Shelbi she continued, "But the stone is old. We need to find new stones again. We need to mine it from its rich core center. You see as the energy is focused through the stone it tends to erode the stone ever so slightly. And over time it's weak in terms of gathering the energy. I don't know why this work for Shelbi and not for me. I know when I was much younger a person, I could pull the energy together and my husband could focus the flow. We never found the third person who could use it to expand and translate it into visions."

Later they would learn that Shelbi has an ancient ancestral link to the planet she doesn't know about and that's why she has the energy the Brendenn needs to amplify to create the majestic thoughts. She has been exposed to the rare chemical at her father's lab during a summer internship. That had altered her genes so she could absorb the energy.

To activate the dormant gene to create the majestic thought they need to find a rare chemical, but they didn't know what it was, yet.

The rest of the afternoon was spent learning more about the fable of how the triangle worked. They asked the Great Grand Nann questions about being naked and learned that was considered one of the secret needs. They talk back and forth amongst themselves how they needed to learn more, practice more and use this rare gift.

They realize that they really needed to find a new raw stone for Shelbi. The priority was to find a source of the mineral and, bring the stones back to the planet for her.

Chapter 15 Rock Name Triangle Game

They arrived the next day to go through the Great Grand Nann's husband's papers. They knew part of the secret was contact between Shelbi and Brendenn.

Shelbi arrived wearing blue shorts, white sneakers and a white tank top. She also had put on her frilly pale-yellow bra and underwear. She wasn't about to get totally naked with Brendenn. But they knew reducing the clothing between their skin helped increase the level and focus of the energy.

Shelbi also thought it was a great way to see Brendenn almost naked. Her desire for a repeat performance of the hospital continue to increase her excitement. She had sworn off doing anything like that again. But hope springs eternal. Someday she'd make love with him not to save his life just for great sex.

Brendenn arrived wearing black shorts, black sneakers and a black T-shirt.

Sabrinna showed up wearing black trousers and a white T-shirt. While a focuser who uses the energy, she didn't believe the skin contact was part of what she needed. Time would prove her to be wrong.

Brendenn sat down in a chair and pulled the chair facing him closer gesturing for Shelbi is sit on it. As she sat down, she felt the stone getting a little warmer. Or perhaps it was her imagination.

After a few minutes Brendenn pulled his chair up closer to Shelbi.

Brendenn spoke first, "The legend says that the warriors of the triangle were naked. Another version says naked to their waists. Let's try the naked to our waists."

"Let's see how Sabrinna gets along with the flow before we strip off." Shelbi countered.

"OK, Shelbi I will wait." Brendenn then turned toward Sabrinna. "Lets us know how you feel the flow."

Sabrinna started looking through the papers that the Great Grand Nann had written. She began to read and absorb and found that strange vision starts to happen as she pulled information together and could see where it would run.

Brendenn again shifted his chair slightly forward so that now Shelbi's legs straddled his left leg.

Shelbi was struggling to stay focused on just being calm. Part of her wanted to reach out and stroke his leg. Part of her wanted him to run his fingers up the back of her calves. Her nipples followed her thinking and began to tingle. *"Or perhaps it's the energy flow,"* she thought.

As Brendenn sat in the chair he too was struggling to focus on the task at hand. Part of him wanted to take his hands and caressed those naked legs. With all the outdoor activities they did together, as part of his therapy they had taken on a honey color not the normal pale white. He found it amazingly attractive almost erotic.

Sabrinna got up and wandered over to a number of books that included old logs from various spaceships. She seemed to be looking for a particular one finally selecting three and returning to the table.

Shelbi was really beginning to focus on Brendenn's physique. Slowly gazing down his T-shirt sleeve she reveled in his toned biceps. She began to fantasize that he was rubbing his fingers over her legs and up the inside of her thighs. The tingling she felt between her legs was nothing to do with the energy it was pure sex.

Brendenn was also feeling the sexual tension. Looking at her neck and the soft skin he wanted to lean forward and start to kiss and nipped at her neck. He could almost smell her womanly scent; the fragrance was intoxicating.

Shelbi realized Brendenn was feeling some of the sexual tension she was. It was obvious that the front of his shorts was now tighter and she could clearly see his manhood imprinted on the front of the elastic. She couldn't help herself as she leaned forward and rested her hands on his warm knees.

Brendenn eyes looked down the top of her tank top. He could see the soft mounds of the top of her breasts and her frilly yellow brassiere. He quickly moved his head to look her in the eyes. Her hands were almost caressing his legs and it was all he could stop to reach out to stroke her bare arms.

Shelbi realized what she was doing and the warmth in her nipples was starting to run down her stomach towards her copper triangle. She sat back and shook her head. It was almost too late.

Brendenn lean forward and ran his fingers gently over her cheeks. He created a tingling sensation that ran down her back and cause goosebumps on her arms.

He saw the goosebumps and his hand roamed down her arm softly caressing them dancing over her skin making them harder. The sensation further hardened her nipples which were now twin points standing out of her tight tank top to his joy.

His hand roamed down her arm and onto her curvy hip. He then slid across the top of her leg caressing it ever so gently. The tingling it set up roamed through her body right to her clitoris. The sensation caused her to clasp her legs together but his knee was in between. She had a greater urge to slide forward and uses leg to satisfy her sexual tension between her thighs.

A fine line of moisture appeared on Brendenn's lip as the sexual tension continued to build. Shelbi also was beginning to pant slightly. She had let go of his knee clasp between her legs. She gripped the chair and wasn't sure how much more she could take before she would straddle him.

Brendenn felt the poking of his manhood and began to think about make love. In his mind he played out her naked body on his. The feeling of entering her warm, slick channel.

Sabrinna meanwhile was unaware of what was going on with the two of them she was reading information and it was scrolling in her mind liked on a tablet screen. She was going back through old logs of battles and she had the feeling she was on the right trail to find out exactly what this miracle mineral was but more importantly where it might be found.

The vision was still cloudy. She needed more energy.

"Shelbi and Brendenn I need more energy. Strip off and let's see what happens."

Shelbi pulled her t-shirt off and then her yellow bra. Brendenn was also striping down taking his black t-shirt off.

Sabrinna felt the energy flow increase. She was warmer and she pulled off her t-shirt and bra. The information was swarming in her head. It was like she was standing on a platform and the pieces of information were swirling around sorting and resorting. She just could not control it yet.

"I still need more energy. I can see things but others are still cloudy. Please you need to get naked."

As Sabrinna finished speaking, she took off her clothes. By the time she finished Shelbi and Brendenn were naked too.

Shelbi could feel the increase in the energy flow rolling over her body. The sexual side was also increasing and her eyes roamed over Brendenn's chiseled chest. She wants to kiss his lips and feel his chest rubbing against her hard nipples. At the same time the energy flow allowed her to feel and not need to move.

Brendenn was in more of a state. The energy was focused and flowing to Sabrinna. He could almost see the pattern in the air between them. His eyes were focused on the naked Shelbi. Part of his mind was off thinking about how much he wanted to caress the soft skin at the top of her breasts. How warm her soft arms would be wrapped around his back.

And then she found it.

"That's it!" Sabrinna yelled, "I've got it I know precisely what the mineral is and exactly the star cluster we will be able to find it. Yes, the mineral is Niarbzium. It is found only in the Aralenn star cluster. That's it. We have to go there that's where it is!"

Her yelling broke the tension between Shelbi and Brendenn. Shelbi quickly strode over to Sabrinna.

"How did you figure this out? How do you know this? Take me through it please."

Sabrinna was now in full vision mode and showed Shelbi the ancient logbooks and a number of charts pushed around on the table. She quickly exclaimed how she arrived and understood exactly what the mineral was based on her reading.

Brendenn was not quite able to move. His manhood had become erect as they stood naked facing one another. If he went over to the ladies, it might be embarrassing to Sabrinna. He was still confused about Shelbi. Maybe she wanted him but maybe not. He would never force himself on her. He'd just have to wait to see.

Shelbi realized she got a narrow escape. Brendenn probably really didn't want to make love to her. Maybe it was just the energy flowing created the situation that they didn't know about. They needed to learn more about their feelings.

Sabrinna sat down. Shelbi pulled the chair up beside her. Brendenn sat across the table from them and they began to plan how get to the galaxy to find out where this mineral might be.

Sabrinna also said she needed to spend more time to see if she could pinpoint it. She needed the two of them there to help.

Shelbi said, "Fine but first I need to go get something to drink. Does anyone else want one?" They both answered yes. She went to the table at the side of the room and pour three glasses of golden orange juice.

Brendenn watched Shelbi naked legs as they gracefully walked to the table. The overall attraction he felt sure was beyond just him wanting the physical side of Shelbi. Still, he hoped she wanted him too.

Chapter 16 Niarbzium Secret Danger

Shelbi's Apple iPad chimed. She noted it was from Sabrinna.

Opening it she saw a message that caused her to stiffen. Code mahogany dark. Room 9230. Now.

Code mahogany was for something that was extremely urgent. Mahogany was an old hardwood that was hard to break. Adding the word dark meant it was a tough problem plus it had something to do with the 3 of them together so Sabrinna could sort information.

She was glad she was wearing her blue lacy bra because she knew that would excite Brendenn. She changed out of her jumpsuit and put on black jeans and a tight white T-shirt.

She arrived at room 9230 noting it was empty. She walked to the back wall and used her left-hand palm on the scanner to open the security door.

As she walked into one of the Campus high security rooms, she noticed Sabrinna was already stripped to the waist. Brendenn was standing on her left side. Shelbi's breath was taken away when she realized that he too was stripped to his waist. Once again, she experienced the rush of arousal looking at his magnificent chest and broad shoulders.

As she pulled off her T-shirt and reached around her back to remove her bra Sabrinna began to talk.

"Sorry for the rush Shelbi. I've had something in the back of my mind I just couldn't put my finger on. About an hour ago I came across this really old logbook in the high-security area. It was in a shipment sent by the Great Grand Nann from her personal collection which arrived yesterday. It's in old dialogue and the writing is actually handwritten. It's really difficult to read. But I think it's very important."

Shelbi walked up to the right side of the lectern and stood looking at Brendenn. A smile crossed his lips as his eyes roamed over her naked upper body.

His eyes ran down the chain with the pendant from Great Grand Nann. He began to imagined it dangling between her breasts while he kissed her warm nipples.

"I just want to lean forward and bury my head in the nape of her neck. I just want to kiss it and smelled that wonderful Shelbi smell. I'd love to hold those wonderful breasts and kiss the tops. Then I could rub my palms over her nipples and make them hard." Brendenn's mind was racing with arousal but he dares not speak out loud.

"I just wanted to trail my fingers across his chest. I want to kiss him so hotly I set his hair on fire. This is getting really difficult not to be aroused." Shelbi's mind was also going into that roll-on-the-floor-sex-is-fun state.

Almost as one they close their eyes. They knew that if they got sexually aroused while it would be interesting and fun it reduces the energy flow. Sabrinna really needed the max flow.

"Is the room getting warmer?" Sabrinna said.

"She must be feeling hot." Shelbi thought, *"because I'm feeling a thin film of moisture starting to rise on my body and not just between my legs."*

Seconds turned into minutes turned into an hour.

Then Sabrinna's voice pierced the silence, "Don't go into the mine without a mask filter! Brendenn it's absolutely critical you don't go in the mine without a mask filter."

"Sabrinna what do you mean?"

"I just figured it out why the Devinn brothers have never been able to channel the energy. The metal releases an invisible gas when it's being mined. It almost as if it protects itself. The invisible gas changes the DNA structure of the people who are mining the stone."

"What do you mean is it changes the DNA. How am is he in danger?" Shelbi asked.

"In reading this 500-year-old diary and translating it the commander whose writing it clearly sets out that when they started to use the mineral, they were fine but when they started to mine it everything changed. The energy cannot flow through to the receiver anymore."

"What does this really mean?" Brendenn asked.

"They can't get the clarity of thought. It may be to protect them so they are not overwhelmed. When they mine it they're surrounded by the stone. If you go into the mine without a filter and inhale the odorless gas you lose the ability to channel the energy from Shelbi"

Brendenn began to process this information.

Shelbi began to talk about the enormous implications. "There are many generations that had been involved in the illegal business. They seem to get dumber over time. Probably it was a reflection of their changed DNA."

"As it is mined it gives off an invisible gas that alters the actual DNA of the miners. It also alters the DNA of anybody who's in the mine. Someone who's just coming to see how the workers are doing, or a foreman all would have their DNA altered."

She paused to let them absorb the information she provided.

"Sabrinna please keep digging in the diary looking at comments and notes, to see if you can find the reason why. We know that the small inverted teardrop that I have has a chip of the stone that could be 1,000 years old. Yet it still is able to focus the energy the Brendenn can pick up and transmit by me. Now imagine if you had an entire chair made of the mineral. The transfer of energy would be enormous."

Again, she paused as both Sabrinna and Brendenn looked down at their chairs and formed a mental picture of the chair made entirely out of the mineral.

"Why it develops the gas I don't know yet. I believe it's to protect the people that are doing the mining. As their mining it they would have enough material to have a huge energy source flow through the person who absorbs it. In fact, if that happens it would actually stop their heart. If somehow it got pass to the person who focuses it their mind could be fried. If it somehow got to the person who has the visions their heart could stop and their mind fried. That's what happened to some of the early people who got involved with large chunks of the mineral after it was mined," Sabrinna said.

Sabrinna paused letting them think about the information. She knew would take a moment to absorb. Clearly, they understood what she was talking about as both of them began to smile.

"That's the reason that the legend has a small inverted teardrop on one of the 3 on the command deck. Big pieces are bad. Mining neutralizes the effect. This explains why the Devinn's who keep mining this can never get the mind expansion results. When they started mining it, it altered the DNA of the people that were doing it which are the family seniors. They probably have large chunks of it in their home. Those large chunks may have some of the raw material around them that's the vein on either side when it's mined. I believe it would continue to give off the gas for a long time."

"It will be imperative that neither of you ever go into the mine. There may be a way to shield from the invisible scent but I haven't discovered that in the diary yet. This explains why people originally were getting the benefits of it stopped."

Sabrinna slumped into a chair. She appeared weary after her explanation. She had been both excited and highly concerned as soon as she learned the information. She knew it was imperative that both Brendenn and Shelbi understood the factor before they got to the planet.

Shelbi broke the silence first, "Thank you Sabrinna. This is very important information. I want to think how this impact our attack strategy."

Brendenn gave out a big sigh, "Yes, it's imperative we understand more about this. But at the moment it's really important that we incorporated into our attack plan."

He began to think of a solution. "Perhaps if we go in with sealed suits and then a decontamination wash of the suits after we may neutralize the impact of the scent. Sabrinna's if you can find information that would support. Meanwhile we will incorporate this new info into our strategy."

"Sabrinna, I want you to keep working on this diary right now. There may be more secrets in it that we need to uncover. Shelbi are you okay for another hour?" Brendenn said.

Shelbi gave out a big sigh. "Brendenn I can stay here as long as Sabrinna needs to tonight. But first I want one hug. Then maybe I can relax. Or Sabrinna can just leave the room and we can . . ."

Both Brendenn and Sabrinna laughed.

"Shelbi I'll gladly give you one hug. But only a quick one or I'm going to be the one asking Sabrinna to leave the room." Brendenn stepped forward and pulled her to his chest. Shelbi gave a little shutter almost a mini climax as she felt Brendenn's warm chest push against her bare breasts and the tightness of his pants press against her belly.

She ran her fingers up his neck and pulled him down to her waiting mouth. For a moment his tongue gentle caressed her parted lips.

Shelbi stepped back. Then she shook her head and closed her eyes saying. "Let's keep working on this cloudy information. There may be more things there that are much more important than rolling around naked with you Brendenn."

The next two and half hours seem to fly by for all three of them. Sabrinna learned more and more about the challenges of actually mining this mineral.

All of this was great information that would avert an amazing disaster if they had move forward without knowing the special gases that altered ones DNA blocking the energy flow.

It would've changed the future of the monarchy on the planet forever and not in a good way.

Chapter 17 Hyperspace Power Reveal

As they hurtled towards the Ryan sector where they knew the Devinns had mining and manufacturing plants on 3 planets, they continue to work on their battle plan.

Brendenn decided he wanted to find out if the power source worked in hyperspace. He told both Shelbi and Sabrinna that he wanted to try the triangle.

They went to the secondary deck of the ship and cleared it of all people and turned off any video feed.

"Okay time to get suited up for action." Shelbi said more firmly than she believed.

She undid her jacket and carefully folded it over a chair. Next, she stripped off her shirt and tie and folded those over the chair. The last garment she took off was her lacy blue bra. Despite being cadet and military her one luxury in life was feminine underwear.

At the same time Shelbi was disrobing the Prince had taken his jacket off and put it on a chair. Stripping off his tie and shirt he was nude to his waist. He flexed his arms a little bit then turned to face Shelbi.

Sabrinna had also disrobed while the other two were shedding their clothes. She took off her T-shirt and slipped out of her frilly yellow bra. One of the things she had in common with Shelbi was an enjoyment of sexy feminine underwear.

She slipped back on the sleeveless vest she had been wearing covering part of her naked breasts.

"Sabrinna, we need to try and focus on which of their mining planets we believe have the mineral. I'd like to have a sense of what we might be getting into," Brendenn said.

He walked over and stood close to Shelbi.

Shelbi looked at his naked chest and couldn't stop her natural reaction. She felt the warmth flow across her chest and down her stomach. Her nipples pebbled slightly.

She cleared her throat. "Brendenn, do you feel any energy surge?"

He reached out and put his hand on her arm. "Yes, I definitely feel that energy pulse. It's not as strong as normal but it's still there."

Moments later Sabrinna chimed in, "There is that feeling. My mind seems to be working in that hyperspace that occurs when that energy flow's. I agree Brendenn it's not as strong as normal but it's still there."

"Hyperspace seems to dilute it but not stop it completely. We will definitely have to investigate more how this works when we get our hands-on new mineral stones," Brendenn said.

Brendenn had let go of Shelbi's arm. He was still standing very close. Shelbi's mind started to wander back to when they had been in the hospital and caressing his body. She closed her eyes so she could focus on where they were and not the feather touch of his fingers on her skin.

Brendenn was also deep in thought. He thought he had been half naked together under control. Clearly, he didn't. As his eyes roamed over Shelbi's naked chest, he has the urge to kiss the tops of her breasts.

"Okay Brendenn focus. It's time to focus on what Sabrinna is doing," He thought.

Sabrinna broke the silence that last.

"Looking at the old diary material and the fresh planet scan we took before we went into hyperspace of the Ryan sector things are sorting themselves out. It's clear the first planet we are going to is the major mining operation. We know that Sebastian Durumann is the VP general manager of operations. He's already told us about that planet and the second planet. For some reason he doesn't have any control over the third planet mining area."

One of the things they learned about the power was that Sabrinna could focus it but it still provided leaps of inspiration from both Shelbi and Brendenn. They really did become a unit of thinking.

"If you look at the movement of that third planet it's shielded most of the time by other planets or asteroids," Shelbi said.

Brendenn then chimed in, "It's interesting that VP Durumann told us a lot about the two planets he's involved with but also let it slip that he is not in charge of the third planet. We know they're doing mining their because they claim they're taking out copper and psyllium."

"Let's focus on the third planet and think about our visit more as a military operation than as a Prince Celebration visit," Brendenn said.

Shelbi asked Sabrinna to throw up a schematic of the planet. Then she began to work out in her mind the military strategy assuming they had to find a hidden mine. She made the assumption that it would not be heavily armed other than protection from Pirates. The Devinns said they had no other security.

They continue for some time and felt they had a good plan in place for when they landed on the third planet.

Then it was time to get dressed. Brendenn took one last longing look at Shelbi's amazing breasts and tantalizing nipples. Similarly, Shelbi glanced at his chiseled chest and let her mind wonder how it would feel to run her fingers over them right now.

All plans are based on knowledge and assumptions. However, they were cadets. Their knowledge didn't extend to the sinister side. The lesson they would learn about evil trickery when they landed could cost them their lives.

Chapter 17 Nice Visit Ends Badly

The ship dropped out of hyperspace as Shelbi's excitement grew. They were going to three different new planets.

The first planet they had contacted the vice president general manager and he was looking forward to the first visit by the Prince. They had asked him to keep it low-key but it did include a review of the facilities and lunch with the senior managers.

They had been given coordinates to land at the mining field. As they emerged from their ship, they notice a number of facilities to service and supply the rockets that left with minerals from the mines.

There was some security but no more than would be expected at a business facility.

The mine tour and luncheon went very well. Everyone was pleasant and very talkative.

When Prince Brendenn engaged the vice president general manager in discussions about the third planet, he said he knew nothing about it. While he had visited the other planet, which was under his control the third planet was controlled by the Devinns family. They specifically told him it was not his concern.

The second planet and mining facility they visited was a similar friendly atmosphere. They were given the coordinates to land. The ship was serviced and supplied. They had the review of the facilities which were quite high tech and efficient.

Then they had dinner with the senior managers and even some of the people who worked on the floor. It was an interesting evening discussing mining and the family's limited support. The conversation turned away from business and they learned some personal things about the various people at the table. Brendenn thoroughly enjoyed it. Shelbi find it interesting but really wanted to move on to the third plant. Sabrinna was her usual friendly self.

Again, he engaged the general manager in a discussion about the third planet. The general manager knew nothing about it and said that it was tightly controlled by the Devinns family for some reason. But since he'd only been on the job three years, he wasn't one to question what was going on.

Brendenn, Sabrinna and Shelbi decided to go out for a night cap.

As they exited the bar, they were surrounded by a group of people who are obviously on a bar hopping journey.

They bumped into Shelbi and Sabrinna as well as bouncing off Brendenn.

As they emerged from the swarm of people Brendenn glanced back at Sabrinna then grabbed Shelbi's hand.

"Come on sweetheart. It's time we got naked again in my room. I just want to bury my head between your naked breasts"

Shelbi looked at him as if he gone mad. But the look in his eye stopped her. His middle finger rose to his lips to signal her to be quiet.

They got to the ship's while Brendenn keep up the chatter of getting naked and planting kisses on various parts of her bare skin continued.

As they arrived at his room and he palmed open the door and Shelbi noticed that Sabrinna had put her back against the wall beside her door but had not entered her room.

As they entered the room Shelbi noticed a small flashing yellow light on a shelf near his bed.

Brendenn put his fingers to her lips for her to be quiet.

Off the shelf he took a small clear box and opened it up. He took a very small device out and put it in his mouth. He then embraced Shelbi and start to kiss down her bare arm. She finds it sensual. He got to a certain point on her arm and stopped. Shelbi felts a pin prick. He sucked on the place and stood up. He spits the device into the box.

"I long to caress your beautiful neck," he said. "I'm going to run my lips across your soft skin while I run my fingers through your copper mound."

He puts his fingers on her lips again and opened a second box putting the small device in his mouth.

He began to loudly kiss her neck as he moved down her skin. Shelbi begins to feel the tension. Her nipples are aroused and she felt a warmth gathering below her copper mound. Again, she felt the vibration in his mouth as he sucked hard on her neck like giving her a love's bite.

He then whips his head back spitting into the box the second device and shutting it quickly.

Sabrinna entered the room and opened a small box similar to what Brendenn had. She popped the little device in her mouth and worked around his neck. Suddenly her head snapped back and she spit something into the box.

She then handed Brendenn a box which he opened up and stuck the small device in his mouth. He began working on her neck. Then his head snapped back and spit into the box Sabrinna held out in her hand.

Sabrinna gathered all four grey boxes up quietly and left the room.

"It's clear some body is after us." Brendenn stated.

Brendenn looked Shelbi in the eye. "You had several nano listening devices implanted on you. They could've implanted by anybody you walk into with the crowd by the bar. We will now provide you with a little scanner so every time you walk into your room you'll know if one's been planted on you. I don't think you're in any danger but I'm not sure."

"I've already called for everyone to return to the ship were going to get out of here in the next 40 minutes."

"Brendenn but it will take at least two hours to get set up in the airport queue so we can fly out of here."

"There are some key perks at being the prince. I can get priority one and get us off the ground in less than 30 minutes if I want to make a commotion. I'll do it in 40 and I think will still make the break without being noticed. Sabrinna is taking those devices and will make sure their strategically placed on the wild cats that are around the spaceport. By the time they finished tracking them and know where they really are, we will be long gone."

Shelbi looked at Brendenn with mixed emotions. This caressing and fondling of her body had her nipples hard. She was slightly wet between her thighs. The serious look on his face and sternness in his eyes stopped her. *Now is not the time for passionate love.* She thought.

Chapter 18 Mining Exploration War

"The coordinates we got for the third planet came directly from Harvard Devinns Senior. I thought that was unusual that a very senior person was providing information but really didn't think much into it," Brendenn said.

When they landed, they were quite surprised. They were the only ship on the field. While there were people there to help refuel and supply them the military presence was extremely heavy.

They were handed an envelope that gave them the coordinates of the mine they could visit.

Brendenn, Shelbi and his protectors thought this was odd since no one was going to escort them. Especially since there was such a heavy military presence at the field.

As Brendenn piloted the vehicle down the route that they had been given he felt uncomfortable.

Shelbi turned to him as she felt the hair standing up on the back of her neck. "There is something odd about this. This people on the field look like mercenaries not family military. I have an uneasy feeling about this. How about you Brendenn?"

"This is very odd. This rumor is the airfield is not been used very much. If we were traveling a normal route, it should be cleaner. I also noted at the field there was no mining exploration buildings or warehousing."

They rose up a long hill. The direction notes this was a long hill and would end in a plateau. That would lead almost directly to the mine road.

As the vehicle came up the plateau, they notice several other vehicles in half circle position It was clear they were not going much further. "Evacuate. Trap." Brendenn yelled. Everyone jumped from the vehicle. They unholster their weapons and moved into formation. It was definitely a mercenary battle.

Brendenn was surgically cut away from his three protectors and Shelbi. Then each of the protectors and Shelbi was separated.

Shelbi had been cut off from the Prince and they were clearly starting to surround him. Uncertain whether he was going to be killed or just captured Shelbi knew she had to slip into warrior mode and figure out how to save Brendenn.

She remembered reading background on the planet how they had strategically placed robotic mechanical suits various places around the planet. Should the miners be attacked the security guards could quickly find a suit rather than having them issued from headquarters.

The trick she had to perform was to find one of those suits, and quickly.

It was also clear in her mind that they were not interested in her since the moment she had been cut off they had turned their attention to Brendenn and ignored the fact she was escaping.

She sprinted along the road that was clearly used as a transportation route. A few minutes later she rounded a corner and spotted the red boxlike shed containing armament. She raced up and wrenched open the door and saw that it was an old MPR 6000 unit.

"Excellent." she said out loud. "This is before biometrics locks, I'm sure I can start this machine."

She quickly opened up the suit slipped her feet into the shoes and leaned back searching for the ignition button. As she suspected it was on the inner left sleeve. Holding it down with her thumb it immediately lit up the suit.

As the suit closed around her, she waited for the screen to come up to tell her about power and ammunition. She thought back to training at the Academy and remembered how several cadets had laughed as she had studied all sorts of old robotic armament.

"You're never going to find anything without biometrics so why bother," a cadet said.

"You never know what kind of planet you're going to be on. You never know when having that tactical information will make a difference. Besides it doesn't hurt to learn as much as you can," Shelbi responded.

The tech screen came online. She found the unit solar panel had kept the power unit at about 85% ready. Ammunition in the right side was at 45% and in the left side at 62%.

"Okay Brendenn, it's time I come and help you knock some heads," Shelbi thought as she activated the machinery and started to jog forward. She jogged slowly at first to get the rhythm and balance of the old machinery. As the rhythm came naturally to her, she began to pick it up the jogging pace.

When she arrived back to where Brendenn was it was clear he was almost surrounded. She decided on a two-prong strategy that she had developed as she was running towards the fight scene.

She quickly targeted two of the mercenaries. She thought of her Cadet training motto, *"Adapt, survive and kill to protect those in need."*

Although wearing armor the mercenaries had not planned for a mechanical armament suit to be part of the battle. Shelbi's quick burst of fire from both the left and the right arm hit and surprised the mercenaries.

She decided Brendenn need to be protected and believe they wouldn't have the firepower to pierce the suit she was wearing. If she was right that would win the battle. If she was wrong, she would go to plan C.

Shelbi strode towards where Brendenn was hunkered down. Then she turned around walking backwards. She quickly cited gun flashes and return fire using double shots not bursts. One found its mark and killed the mercenary.

She backed up to where Brendenn lay prone in the sand. She could see several shots had grazed his body. One in his left shoulder and left arm. One grazed the calf on his right leg.

She realized that there wasn't any gunfire for several seconds and quickly scanned the area. No gun flashes. As she expected they were communicating. They would be considering plan A retreat or plan B cluster and have a large frontal attack.

She stood with guns ready and found they had selected plan B.

Blazing shots appeared from one focal point.

"That's a strategic error. Strategic errors lose battles," Shelbi remembered from her tactical class.

While bullets were whizzing around her, they were being deflected by the armor. She planted her left foot behind her and raise both arms and blazed away with a gun flash. After spending 10% of her ammunition, she stopped.

All was quiet. There was no returning fire or flashes. Off to the left Shelbi telescoped the helmet eye piece and saw a black object coming in, clearly a helicopter. It swooped down and she could see people running towards it. They had moved to Plan A, retreat and evacuate the area.

At the same time several other military helicopters showed up. The markings indicated this was the prince's military group. Soldiers repelled out of the helicopters surrounding the mercenary's vehicle.

Shelbi turned and knelt beside Brendenn while popping open her faceplate.

"Shelbi? Shelbi is that really you?" Brendenn exclaimed.

"This is another fine mess you got us into Brendenn. Of course, I had to be the one to save your…,"

"Sorry about that. I don't think this one's going to end with us naked together in the dirt here."

"You're partly right Brendenn. We are certainly not going to be naked here in the dirt. Let's focus on getting you fixed up again." She continued the thought. *"Someday I'm going to find somewhere for you to be naked."*

Chapter 19 Prince Valley View Reward

Shelbi and Sabrinna stepped off the ship and walked down the long slopping grey ramp towards Brendenn. He was waiting beside a long black limousine to go to his home.

Almost 2 months had gone by and Shelbi was back to his home planet to finish her strategic paper research.

Sabrinna was there to help her on understanding some of the old diary information on strategies used in several successful historical galaxy wars.

Brendenn asked Shelbi to make sure she had three spare days. He said he had something special he wanted to share with her.

He had taken them both to his large home. Shelbi had gone to her usual bedroom and unpacked. After a nice lunch she set out to visit with the Great Grand Nann.

Shelbi walked into the living room and noted the Great Grand Nann was sitting on the sofa near the sitting chair. A service with tea and a tray of cookies were in front of her.

"I knew you were coming and I have some wonderful black tea that I know you mentioned the last time were here you really like. I understand you have some questions. I'll try to help," the Great Grand Nann said.

"First Great Grand Nann I want to give you your heritage necklace. I finished doing the research on my strategic paper. Thank you very much for loaning it to me. It was really helpful when I was working with Brendenn and Sabrinna."

With that Shelbi stood up reach behind her neck and unclipped the class. Great Grand Nann stood up and turned her back to Shelbi.

"Would you please be so kind as to slip it on and attach it behind my neck."

"Great Grand Nann it would be my pleasure," Shelbi said.

For the rest of the afternoon they sipped tea, ate cookies and had a wonderful discussion on many of the questions that Shelbi had. Her research had given her a tremendous amount of information. However, there were just some final points that only the Great Grand Nann with her personal experience could fill in.

The next morning Shelbi got up early. She packed a small overnight bag, did her morning bathroom duties and slipped downstairs for a quick breakfast. As arranged at 8:30 she was standing by the front door of the house. Brendenn pulled up in a sleek blue air cruiser.

Shelbi took her overnight bag and carried it to the vehicle by Brendenn. He smiled at her and said, "I hope you're going to enjoy this I want to share with you something very special. Actually, it all started with my grandfather."

"What is it exactly were going to see?"

"No more questions Shelbi just trust me."

The vehicle soon exited the city and ended up going along the route beside the sea. Shelbi began to relax and just enjoy the magnificent scenery of this planet. She hadn't experienced much of it most of time she'd been doing research or involved with the Prince and his adventures.

After several hours they came into the foothills of the mountains. Shelbi had seen pictures of them but never experienced just how awe inspiring they were.

Tall and rugged she knew several of the interior mountain summits actually had snow caps.

As they turned off the road and came up to a magnificent stone gate with a ranger standing beside the entrance. The prince stopped before the close gate.

The ranger exited the hut and using a wand scanned the vehicle. A smile broke over his face.

"Welcome back Prince Brendenn. This is your friend Cadet Shelbi MacPhadden. I don't need to see any id. Tech scan has identified you. The garage for your vehicle is open and will be secured when you leave."

Brendenn turned right and drove for a short way coming up to a building the blended into the mountain area with its reflective glass architecture. He parked the vehicle in the garage.

They walked around the garage to a small cabin. The prince walked in carrying his overnight bag as did Shelbi. Just as they entered the door Shelbi noted that there were two pairs of riding boots just inside the front door.

"Here's a pair of riding boots for you Shelbi. Go into that bedroom over there and you'll find a pair of riding pants you can wear. We are going to be riding on horseback and those shorts you are wearing won't be comfortable."

Moments later Shelbi emerged in the new black leather riding boots and brown riding britches. Still carrying her overnight bag, she walked outside and found Brendenn beside one of three magnificent horses. He helped her into the saddle of the brown horse while he himself got on the brown and white Palomino. Their bags were secured on a third horse the Brendenn held the leather led to.

As they walked up the trail Brendenn began to tell Shelbi the history of this beautiful area.

"My grandfather bought this land over 100 years ago. He wanted as a family retreat so we could enjoy nature. He wanted us to remember that it wasn't all regal ceremony, and manufacturing, it was about real people in real places. We're going up to the small family cabin that he and my dad built. It overlooks one of the most magnificent valleys in the whole area."

For the next couple of hours, they ambled with Brendenn pointed out various sites to Shelbi. She began to understand that some of these magnificent trees were hundreds of years old. Their leaves were spectacular colors. Some were orange and green and even reds. Brendenn had told her in the fall they change colors become yellows and oranges and purples.

They reach the base of a large mountain and the trail became narrow. Brendenn said he would go first and Shelbi could follow.

After climbing for over an hour they rounded a corner and Shelbi's breath was taken away. A magnificent valley with rolling dark green trees and yellow grass laid out before her.

They went along a little further and came to a beautiful wooden structure.

"This is your small family cabin?" Shelbi said with amazement. The structure was two-stories and made out of huge wooden logs. A massive covered porch ran around 3 sides. It had to be well over 3,000 square feet

"Yes, at the other end of the valley we have the other family cabin with 10 bedrooms, four fireplaces and a table that will seat 25. So yes, this is the small cabin."

As they walked inside Shelbi was amazed at how beautiful the wood interior was. Large tree logs held up the second floor. A curved wooden stair of with red and white steps led to the bedrooms. A floor to ceiling stone fireplace was on the wall of the living room.

"Before we settle down let's take the horses to the corral and give them a good rub down," Brendenn said as he put down the two overnight cases.

They went outside and took the horses to the corral. Shelbi took the saddle and blanket off her horse and began to rub it down. Brendenn performed a similar exercise on the other horses.

They went back inside and Brendenn took Shelbi's bag up to the second floor.

He walked into a bedroom and smiled.

"This used to be my bedroom. You can use it while we are here overnight. It has one of the best views of the valley. The sun will come up on the left side of your bed. You can watch it as it walks across the mountains."

"And were you going to sleep?"

"There's a new master bedroom that's been built on the main floor. My parents have one on one side of the cabin and they created one for me on the other side. I haven't slept in it yet. This is the first time I've been here since it's been finished."

The rest of the day was spent relaxing, eating, and drinking wine. They sat on the porch until the sun set and it began to get cool.

Near the end of the evening with the wine making her feel mellow Shelbi looked at Brendenn and realized how she wanted the evening to play out. She looked at his biceps as he picked up the glass and began to imagine his soft fingers trailing over her arms. The lips that were touching his glass kissing her soft ruby lips.

Brendenn was also realizing that what started out as a just come see my valley trip was certainly creating a different feeling as Shelbi sat beside him. His eyes roamed over her legs and began to think about what it would be like to caress them.

He'd seen her semi naked often enough the longing was beginning to rise his manhood.

He turned his head and focused on his climbing tree and thought about it as a child. That actually didn't help. He decided he better move and go to bed before he began to make passionate love to her there on the porch.

Shelbi reluctantly went upstairs. The more she thought about Brendenn the more aroused she became. Her nipples were feeling warm and that warmth was spreading down her belly. The tension was building in her thighs and she knew she had to do something about it.

As she stood in her cadet T-shirt, she stripped off her pajama bottoms and threw them on the bed. Her palms rubbed her rising nipples through her T-shirt. They began to pebble and feel needy.

She decided to see if Brendenn was still awake. This was the perfect opportunity for them to take all the sexual tension they'd had and enjoy it in this wonderful atmosphere.

Shelbi patted silently bare foot down the curved wooden stairs. As she walked towards his room she thought, *"If he's in bed asleep I'll just turn around and go back to my room. I can always pleasure myself."*

As she walked toward his room, she passed the main hall and saw the door to the front porch was open. She looked and saw him standing by the door wearing a pair of silver pajama bottoms. The moonlight lit up his toned shoulders.

She walked over and leaned up on his left side.

Brendenn's arm went around her shoulder and squeezed it.

He turned towards her and she rose on her toes, her hand behind his head and pulled him in for a kiss.

She kissed him lightly. A quick kiss that he could feel the passion behind.

She pressed against his stomach and she could feel his manhood rise.

Shelbi wanted to feel his warm skin against her breasts now! She walked over to a chair, shed her T-shirt and folded it on the chair back.

She walked back and crushed her breasted into his hot chest feeling the warmth of his body roll over her. She breathed deeply of his manly scent.

His fingertips gently caressed her bare back leaving a trail of goose bumps.

"I love the way her skin pebbles as a I lightly drag my fingers over her," Brendenn thought.

Shelbi leaned back so just the tips of her nipples were touching his hot flesh. Then she leaned in and licked first his right nipple than his left nipple. She moved back to the right nipple and began to suck it as she felt him shudder. His manhood was now hard, firmly pressed against her belly.

"I can't believe how amazing her hot lips feel on my nipples," Brendenn thought as Shelbi continued to caress them

"I'm going to kiss every inch of your lovely body before I have my way with you Shelbi," Brendenn said. Then he leaned in and kissed her passionately on the lips.

He could stand it no more. He picked her up and strode to his bed. She could feel his need pressed against her thigh as he carried her.

He laid her naked body on the bed with her head on his white pillow. As he stepped back, he thought, *"The moonlight flits across your body and makes it look really sensuous."*

"I will have my way with you in just the moonlight, my love," Brendenn said.

As he talked to her, she could feel the heat roll off her breasts and plunge down her belly and rolling between her thighs. She was becoming hot and eager for his tongue to caress her.

Brendenn undid the drawstring of this pajama bottom raised it up over his hardness and dropped it to the floor.

Shelbi moved to the center of the bed to give him room to lie down beside her.

As he laid down his head came down to her right breast and blew warm breath over her right nipple hardening it even more. Then he began to flick it with the end of his raspy tongue. A shiver ran over her, shaking her flesh.

She ran her fingers down his belly and grasped his rigid rod. *"My he really is big. I know it's going to be some pain and then pleasure when I get an inside me."*

Brendenn had now moved over to her left breast and began to lick and suck her nipple. She pushed her breast into his face as her fingers intertwined the hair at the back of his neck. She pulled him harder. Then his face crushed her breast while his tongue continued to flick her nipple back and forth in a fast rhythm.

He rose up and began to slowly kiss down her belly. When he got to her navel, he flecked it eagerly with his warm tongue and then move quickly to the sensuous copper patch above her vagina.

He sat up on his right elbow and used his left hands to stroke the copper hairs. Then he began to curly the hair into his fingers and tugged at it irritating her bud.

She ran her fingers over his stomach and watched his reaction as he felt the pleasure.

"I really love the way I can give him pleasure. The way it provides me pleasure also is just amazing," Shelbi thought.

In one swift movement he was between her legs kissing the inside of her thighs over and over again.

She grabbed his head and tried to pull it up so he would work his magic on her vagina lips. But he resisted and kept kissing the insides of her thighs. Then he was nipping at them with his sharp teeth.

Her vagina lips were fully engorged, wet and eager to feel his tongue.

She ran her fingers around his ears knowing how much he loved it. It drove him over the edge and he brought his warm tongue to her wet vagina.

His tongue slowly rose up and down.

"Her love juice taste so sweet," He thought to himself as his tongue continued to work its magic.

Shelbi was squirming now and again tried to pull his head up to impale her lower lips with his tongue.

"If he doesn't take me soon, I'm just going to explode naturally," She thought

Brendenn cupped her bottom with both hands and pushed her slowly away and began kissing her legs again.

"No, you can't do that I need you now," Shelbi exclaimed.

He smiled and returned his tongue rolling over her wet clitoris. As he alternated his tongue moving inside her slick nether lips, then sliding up and over clitoris, she was beginning to rhythmically move back and forth.

"Don't stop! I'm so close and I need to come," Shelbi said.

He bore down on his clitoris with his lips sucking it back in to his mouth and flecking it mercilessly with his hot tongue. Shelbi's legs crushed around his head and she grabbed his hair as the heat rose and she began to climax shaking back and forth against him.

When at last she had stopped shaking with passion he reared back and began to kiss slowly up her belly.

"Oh no my love, it's my turn," Shelbi said.

She pushed him on his back and flipped her right leg over his right leg.

Her lips now came down on his nipples but rather than suck them she began to bite them causing him pain and pleasure.

"You little minx. You know I won't be able to control myself if you keep doing that."

Shelbi's hand reached down and grabbed his rigid manhood. She felt the thin film that he had managed to somehow cover it with. She knew he wanted to have protection and she hadn't even seen him put it on.

She moved her lips down and encircled the head of his rising manhood despite being covered she could taste the saltiness. She encircled it and began to rhythmically bob her head up and down.

His arms came down and grabbed her pulling her up his chest dragging her nipples across the hair surface. Already tense and sore from his sucking the sensation shudder through Shelbi.

Laying down on him she rose up and rubbed her clitoris up-and-down his rigid manhood. Faster and faster, she moved her hips crushing her breasts into his chest at the same time.

Brendenn spread his legs to allow her to get even closer and ran his fingers up and down her back feeling the soft skin. Finally, he could stand it no more he grabbed her backside and pushed her hard against him. Seconds later Shelbi shattered with her second body shaking climax.

Her legs trembled as that her whole body lay tight against him. Her arms were along his shoulders holding her tight to them.

She sat up on his thighs and traced her fingers over his toned muscles. As her fingers began to flick his nipples, he picked her up and slowly put the head of his manhood in her dripping vagina.

He kept moving in the lubricated channel and out again.

Shelbi tried to push down but he was too strong and kept holding her back.

She held her breast in one hand and he began to suck on the nipple. As his hands left her hips, she quickly impaled herself on his pulsating manhood.

As she pushed harder and harder, he filled her completely stretching her with a little pain but more pleasure. When he was fully inside her she stopped. He continued to alternate sucking first one nipple then the other while kneading her breasts.

Slowly she began the rhythmic dance to bring him to the height of his pleasure. He crushed her to his chest and began the rhythmic dance in and out of her slick wetness.

At last, their rhythm matched each other and the pace picked up.

As he reached his climax, he drove deep inside her and held her down she felt the warmth pressing against her vagina. She also climaxed at the same time in her legs shattered as she felt him pumping.

She lay on top of him amazed that having climaxed he was still filling her completely. As he rolled onto his side hugging her, she stayed tight against him. He pulled slowly out of her sore pulsating vagina.

Together they lay with the moon playing across their bodies. Her fingers continued to dance across his skin giving them the pleasure that only to lovers can enjoy.

Shelbi knew in the morning they would have to leave.

"Thank you Brendenn, for the valley and giving of yourself." Brendenn smiled as Shelbi whispered the words in his ear.

Chapter 20 New Stone Power

Sabrinna was excited as she opened the special grey security box. Inside were 3 different coloured jewelry boxes. Each one contained a new gold necklace similar to the Great Grand Nanas except these were attached to a recently mined Niarbzium teardrop pendant.

After they found the mine for the Niarbzium mineral Sabrinna wanted to find out what level of energy could be generated by a new stone. She wondered how that would affect her vision abilities.

Also, she wondered what would happen if Shelbi, Brendenn and her each worn a stone. What would that create for each of them?

The next day the three of them met in a secure Academy room.

Shelbi walked in and seeing the two of them already inside close the door and palmed the security lock. All three of them began to take off their tops. Shelbi unclasped her frilly blue bra and carefully folded in on the chair where her white shirt has been draped. Sabrinna laughed as she noticed that she too had the same frilly blue bra as Shelbi. They really did think alike.

Brendenn looked at Shelbi's beautiful breasts and his thoughts drifted back to their time in the valley. *"This has to be the tough's part of this whole process. Seeing those beautiful naked breasts with those strawberry-like nipples I just want to kiss and caress."*

"That amazing chiseled chest. I just want to run my fingers over his back while my lips caress his manly skin. I'd love to press my breasts against his stomach and feel his manhood rise against my bare tummy," Shelbi thought.

They both shook their heads, looked away and came back to the task at hand.

Sabrinna handed Shelbi the blue jewelry box and Brendenn the black jewelry box.

Shelbi opened it and felt a little warmth spread across her. Brendenn reached out taking the gold chain out of the blue jewelry box and slip it on Shelbi's neck, attaching the clasp.

He then turned to Sabrinna and took the necklace out of her red jewelry box and fastened it around her neck.

Brendenn knelt down and Shelbi put his necklace around his neck.

"There's a heat spreading across my breasts. It is making my nipples tingle but it's not really sexual," Sabrinna said.

Shelbi was also feeling the impact of the stone dangling between her breasts. Using her arms, she squeezed the stone between her breasts and felt the warmth spread across. She knew this was the bonding process the stone would go through. It was much stronger than the time she'd borrowed one from the Great Grand Nan. In fact, it was not only spreading across her chest but it seemed to rise up her neck and spread around her head.

Sabrinna grabbed onto the back of her chair and gulped in fresh air almost panting with the impact of the stone energy as it spread.

"There's so much information swirling around. I'm going to have to find something to focus on. The energy flowing is just amazing," Sabrinna said.

Brendenn had been quiet while the two of them appeared to be adjusting to the stones bonding. He too felt the surge of heat across his chest and down his stomach.

As he stood in front of Shelbi, he felt the energy flowing over them. It was much, much stronger than before. It seemed to be very focused on streaming to Sabrinna. Before she wore the stone, it seemed to just flowed over and around her. Now he could almost see blurring line of energy. It was almost like a stream of light traveling to her.

Sabrinna had brought along one of the old captain's logbooks covering a famous battle. The strategies had been used in classrooms and discussed for years. Why the ancient warriors had used the strategies and how they evolved had always been a mystery. Anyone who reviewed the data and looked at it felt they were making huge mistakes. But they won the battle despite the fact. No one could ever figure out why.

She looked at the data and instantly became involved in watching it float around her. She began to sort it and saw quickly a number of flaws that were in the original battle plan and then followed it as it evolved. She could see how they would do moves that they made no sense except to someone who had the energy and could feel the flow was right.

They formed a triangle in the room Sabrinna holding the book at one corner. Shelbi facing Brendenn in another. Brendenn looked at the two of them and despite the energy flow between them felt the warmth spreading over his body he hadn't felt before.

Shelbi stripped off her pants and lacy blue underwear and stood naked. She felt this was important for the energy gathering. She was right as she was about to learn.

Brendenn followed by taking his clothes off. It had a slightly different reaction for him. He realized looking at Shelbi's naked body that part of him was detached and moving into the area of sexual excitement. His manhood was definitely responding to seeing her naked body. He placed his hands strategically to support himself and remained quiet.

Sabrinna had joined them stripping off her pants and underwear. She felt now like the energy was enfolding her like a complete capsule. She had never felt it so strong. It was amazing to feel the power.

As she looked at the battle plan in the old log book, she began sorting alternatives. She began seeing with amazing speed the ones that would be obvious but wouldn't work in a total flow of the battle.

As she continued to look at the battle and see how it unfolded, she felt she had learned everything she could about it from using the log book.

As she closed the book a new idea rolled into her evaluation sphere. She began to gather information hidden in her mind that she had read about the Devinns. She quickly focused on a contract they had with the Erbecton group. She had spent the last month reading many of their contracts to fully understand what they were up to in their evil ways.

Meanwhile Shelbi was starting to feel the effects of looking at Brendenn's naked body. Her eyes ran up his legs and she began to think about the manhood slipping between her hot thighs. As the heat from the energy folded over her entire body it was also replaced with a sexual tingling that had her nipples tense. It was almost like a second ribbon of energy running down to her copper mound. She could feel her clitoris starting to be needy.

"Perhaps if I just run my fingers over his chest and give him a kiss that will satisfy my needs," Shelbi thought.

Brendenn began to feel a secondary flow from Shelbi that wasn't the usual energy flow but had a sexual tinge to it. It was definitely creating a hardness between his thighs. His hands were now on top of the one another in order to cover his ridged manhood.

"I don't know how long Sabrinna needs but my needs are getting stronger and stronger. I just want to kiss Shelbi's breasts and then work my way done to her rosebud below her copper mound. I want to run my tongue over her lower lips and suck on her hot nub."

Suddenly Shelbi felt the stone between her breasts begin to vibrate. As it settled down, she had a new link to Sabrinna that bypass Brendan. She felt like she was standing beside her watching her gather information and sort things.

"It must be part of the stone link since were now both have them. I wonder if I can at least communicate with Sabrinna?" Shelbi thought.

"Yes Shelbi, I can hear you. I can see you standing beside me. I don't think you're going to be able to manipulate data that you can see but perhaps you can spot something that I'm missing."

Sabrinna was sorting alternatives and beginning to do a little dance with her hands waving in the air. It was almost like she was sorting material and pulling it in and then throwing it out.

At first Shelbi was overwhelmed by all the data. But then she began to see clusters of information with a link through Sabrina's eyes. She began to think about strategy rather than just data gathering.

Then Shelbi spotted something that got her attention. There appeared to be a significant movement of the mineral to the Erbecton Group. More than they could possibly use to build energy needs on the planet. From a strategic point of view, she knew that this could also be used for military weapons. She asked Sabrina to start digging into other data she might be able to see now that she had identified the dangerous trend.

As Sabrinna continued sorting information, she saw a small company division set up for military energy purposes. In fact, the more she sorted the data a strategy became clear that Devinns and Erbecton group was going to make a run for authority and take out the existing King.

Sabrinna began to sort out the true danger of the Devinns and Erbecton Group working together. Shelbi helped by identifying the three different approaches they might take to attack the King and Queen. She also saw how then Devinns would then take control. She then began to work at finding alternative ways to head off the danger.

Shelbi pulled up an image screen and began to quickly add the information she had so she would be able to discuss it with Brendenn.

With Sabrinna gathering data and looking at various elements faster than she could absorb the information Shelbi turned her attention back Brendenn.

Sabrinna observed the Brendenn and Shelbi had a sexual side she didn't have. "*It must be a loop between them*," she thought.

"With all the information flowing around in the energy swirling and pulling the data and information I must be too focused for me to worry about the physical side. Because it's flowing through the other two, they have time to think about the physical aspects of being naked."

Shelbi realized she had control of gathering of the energy more with the added power of the new stone. She pulled the sexual energy out as layer over the core energy flowing to Brendenn.

"Brendenn, see if you can manage the secondary sexual flow somehow not to go to Sabrinna but loop back to me. It would increase the energy flow she needs."

"Yes, I can feel it now. I think I can maneuver it. Let me try to control it. Shelbi just goes with the flow."

Brendenn began to think about using the energy to surround just the two of them. He examined the bubble and thinned out the energy. It seems to increase the flow of core energy.

They both realized at the same moment that the inner sexual feeling was stronger. They felt like they were near a climax the feeling were so intense. As the energy feeling rose it had the opposite impact on their physical being. Shelbi felt her nipples relax. Brendenn's manhood also dropped. They were at a different level of sexuality.

They realized this was how they could be in battle mood, channel the energy and still be sexually aroused. It seems to focus and speed up the channeling of the core energy. Physically they did not have to worry about what others saw.

Suddenly, Shelbi felt tired and the stone between her breasts grew cool. The tingling of the energy seemed to slow swirling around her. However, the sexual tension was still high.

Brendenn also felt the cooling process. Like Shelbi the sexual side focused on his manhood became more urgent.

"When we finish here Shelbi perhaps you and I could go for it a drink or a light dinner?" Brandon said.

"Brendenn, as long as it's in your room you can have anything you want to caress oops, I meant eat, no-no drink. Oh, what the heck as long as we can get naked together."

Sabrinna was tired but there is some urgency to the information she had discovered.

"Brendenn, Shelbi and I have discovered the King and Queen are in grave danger. We have seen the Devinns and the Erbecton Group plotting to over throw them. We need to use Shelbi's strategy skills to save them."

As Sabrinna talked the other two were very focused on what she was saying. It shook Brendenn to his core. With the right energy weapons, the Devinns and the Erbecton Group could over throw the King and Queen.

"I need to rest before we have another session. You two take care of your other needs come back after."

"Actually Sabrinna, we can take care of our needs in the triangle flow. Let's just relax and eat some food then continue, if you are up to it," Shelbi said.

Sabrinna agreed. They gathered some food and sat naked eating. They all knew their lives would change forever with the next session.

Chapter 21 Shelbi's Special Award

Shelbi had just finished recording her daily log as her cam pinged. She touched the screen and Sargent McDonald from the commander's office appeared. He was wearing full dress uniform.

"Cadet Shelbi your presence is requested in the commander's office now. Please wear your parade dress uniform."

"Yes sir. Should I make it on the double?" Shelbi asked.

"That won't be necessary cadet Shelbi. But we need to see you smartly."

Shelbi knew smartly meant not to waste time but she didn't need to run.

She walked in the office and the Sargent rose to his feet. He gave her a smart salute. She stopped turned to face him, and saluted back.

"Please go right in Cadet Shelbi MacPhadden."

The door to the commander's office was open, Shelbi entered and stopped abruptly.

There is sitting in the chair was Brendenn.

As she entered the commander stood as did Brendenn and faced her. Both were in dress uniforms. Each gave her a salute. She stopped, came to attention, and saluted them.

"At ease cadet Shelbi MacPhadden. Please take the chair to the right of Brendenn."

Shelbi wasn't sure why she was being called or why Brendenn was there but she thought silence was the best tactic.

The commander smiled and looked directly at Shelbi.

"Cadet Shelbi I'm very pleased to inform you that you are going to receive the Jeffrey Humanitarian Award. As you may remember the Jeffrey Humanitarian Award is provided to an outstanding member of the military that's made a significant impact on an alien culture. Brendenn has just come from the final review of the award committee. He submitted your application several weeks ago. For the last hour they been questioning him. They then asked him to leave the room for their voting. He came immediately to tell me that it was animous. All 11 members voted for you. This is a major precedent. No one that is not on active duty has ever received this award let alone a cadet."

Shelbi was taken aback. This was an amazing award and she never ever expected to achieve it let alone as a cadet.

She now understood why the salute when she entered the office was provided. It was their way of making this a formal situation.

"Commander I'd like to thank you very much for your support of this application. It's an amazing award. Brendenn I'd like to thank you very much for the honor and your support."

The commander smiled and sat back in his chair. "Cadet Shelbi what you did for Brendenn and his people was amazing. Your focus on the war strategy, your discovery of the elements of over throwing the King and Queen, and then working with Brendenn and

Sabrinna to devise a strategy to outwit the Devinns was outstanding."

Shelbi smiled and colored slightly. She felt no remark was necessary.

The commander looked at Brendenn, "I'm going for coffee you have 22 minutes."

He rose from his chair and came around his desk heading to the door. As his hand touched the door handle, he turned back to Brendenn, "Cadet Brendenn you have the room."

Brendenn smiled at Shelbi and walked over to the bookcase. He palmed open the security room behind it.

Shelbi thought, *"Here we go again. I wonder what all this is about?"*

She followed Brendenn into the secure room and sat in the chair he motioned to. When the door shut, he began to speak.

"Shelbi today it is official and will be announced in the morning. I wanted you to have a heads up on what's happening back on my world with the Devinns family. Your insightful strategic insights worked perfectly. We took them without any real battle or loss of life. The father and two sons have been put on house arrest for life. They will be allowed to leave the planet but only to go to another planet that is nothing to do with manufacturing, military or any business. They will not be allowed to participate in any business again."

Brendenn paused to allow the message to sink in to Shelbi.

When she didn't speak, he continued. "I intervened so that the family wasn't stripped of everything. The family will be allowed to continue on with their manufacturing, trade and export business. The mine however, has been confiscated, the distribution of the minerals and the military support awarded to my family."

"The Devinns family for years has been mining the element and turning it into liquid silica then poured into molds. Turning it into liquid destroyed its molecular structure. Another reason why they could never find the energy focus."

"They had been selling it illegally to other cultures who did use it for energy. But not the energy that created the triangle. We will honor those contracts that are not military in order to keep relationships with the various groups."

Brendenn reached down to a briefcase beside his chair and opened it up taking a small package out of it.

"Shelbi, on behalf of a grateful nation I would like to provide you the small token of our appreciation."

Shelbi took the blue box and undid the yellow ribbon. When she opened the box up, she saw a beautiful gold band. Taking it out she saw a designed in the shape of a triangle in a circle on it. She slipped it on her left wrist and noticed a dark black chip in the band.

"Thank you Brendenn I really appreciate this. What is the Blackstone?"

"That's a chip of the Niarbzium mineral with a high core rating. We thought that you should have that forever. We understand you won't be part of the triangle again but we still wanted you to have this is a sincere appreciation of what you did for us."

Shelbi smiled. She was very appreciative of the gold band and the fact that it contained that special mineral Niarbzium. She glanced towards Brendenn and saw he was very focused on her.

"I think I know what's going through your mind Brendenn you're wondering if this is going to be a stronger energy focus now that I'm wearing this. We both know that as a cadet I'm not allowed to wear this except on casual situations. So, the good news is you don't have to worry about me walking around with it. But I'm sure you want to grab my buns and find out what the feeling is."

With that said she rose out of the chair and walked towards Brendenn. He rose out of his chair and walked over and just as his hand reached out to grab her left cheek the secure door slid back and Sabrinna stepped into the room.

"I couldn't wait any longer this is so amazing. The Jeffrey Humanitarian award congratulations Shelbi. Oh, I'm sorry you just gave her the bracelet didn't you. Oh well perhaps I've saved you again Brendenn."

Shelbi and Brendenn laughed heartily.

"He's still needs to find out what it's like Sabrinna. Come and join us and we'll see how the bracelet works now."

Shelbi leaned her breast against Brendenn's warm chest. Sabrinna came over and stood beside them. Brendenn grabbed Shelbi's right butt cheek and danced her up on her toes. He then let go and stepped back.

Sabrinna was shaking her head. "We're going to have to learn more about this mineral. That was a much stronger flow of energy. What do you think Brendenn?"

"Yes, that was definitely a bigger surge of energy."

Brendenn sat back down and Shelbi realized he had more to talk about.

"Shelbi what I'm about to tell you now can never leave this room. No one can know for least several months. My family is endowing a large sum of money form the mining company to build a research facility on our home planet. It will be finished in about 2 years. At that time Sabrinna is going to take over as its managing director."

"I hate to interrupt," Shelbi said, "but I thought she was your lifetime protector?" She glanced at Sabrinna as she said this.

"Yes, however finding out how this mineral works, getting together a collective group of triads is much more important than my life. Well not quite. But she already has the most experience of anyone on the planet with dealing with the focusing of the energy. We can find receivers, channelers, and seers to fully discover the potential of what this really can provide, but we need to have someone who can lead the research that really understands how it feels and how works. In order to continue her role until that time it's imperative that no one knows she's going to do that."

After some more chitchat a small ding was heard. Sabrinna's stood up, "That's 22 minutes time to go."

Shelbi was exhausted by the day's events and headed off to her room for much needed sleep.

Chapter 22 Warrior Graduation Celebration

It was a week before graduation and Shelbi had just finished a free style work out. As she walked back towards her room, she saw Sabrinna standing near her door.

"Sabrinna how nice to see you. How can I help you?"

"I know that you and Brendenn after graduation are getting together. He's having the Royal suite at the Skagway hotel in the convention center where all the celebrations will be. It's a three-bedroom unit. I just want you to know that I will be there along with my date in a bedroom as part of his protection. I didn't want you walking out naked in the middle of the night to get a glass of water and be surprised by me or my date."

"Sabrinna thanks for telling me. I actually hadn't thought about the security part."

"The issue is that last year four graduate students decided to test their ability and the Prince's security. Yes, they did manage to abduct him for about 35 seconds. But they didn't realize the seriousness of what they were doing. Now it's an unofficial report."

An unofficial report meant that it was noted in the commander's log but not on their personal school records.

"What they don't know is they now have been tagged for life. Should they ever come to a planet that the Prince is on they will immediately be monitored. If two or more appear at the same time they will be taken in for a discussion."

After little more talk Sabrinna went off and Shelbi put her out of her mind. As she lay down to go to sleep, she began to think that Brendenn's life was more complicated than she realized. She also realized how special the time was when they were just the two of them in the Valley.

The graduation ceremony was amazing. Each cadet year had its own auditorium. Shelbi sat with 700 other graduates. They all listen to the speech by the commander. She had been called to the front to accept her Jeffrey humanitarian award and given her 92 second thank you speech. And now she was back at her room.

It was a huge convention center and there would be a lot of partying that night. It would start with each year going to its appointed ballroom for their individual dance, buffet and general celebrations. As the night wore on, they would spill out into the corridors and by morning many of the various year cadets would be intermingled.

Shelbi looked at the bed where she had laid out her light blue dress, blue frilly bra, and marching lacey underwear. She knew it was both the colour and style the Brendenn really liked. The dress was short enough that it covered the essential parts of her body but still allowed her graceful toned legs to appear.

As she walked towards her shower, she began to think of spending time with Brendenn alone.

She put her cadet suit in the fresher and was standing naked in the bathroom. She ran her hands over her sides thinking of Brendenn's hot lips.

She noticed that her nipples began to pucker just thinking about him kissing them and flicking them with his tongue. As the warmth traveled down her belly to her copper mound, she ran her fingers through it. She could hardly wait for Brendenn to do the same and give it a playful tug. As the heat began to build between her thighs, she thought she better get in the shower and stop thinking. She wondered, *"what Brendenn was up to?"*

Brendenn was in a similar state of mind. He had put his formal cadet dress suit in the fresher. He was thinking about the fact that he.

He stood in his birthday suit and thought about what he hoped would happen that night. He was looking forward to the big graduation celebration and food buffet. Even more he was looking at gathering up Shelbi and taking her to the hotel room.

Brendenn's mind wandered back to their time in the mountains. He remembered her lying naked on the bed with the moonlight on her body. She had those amazing pebbly nipples.

He began to think about kissing the tops of her warm breasts. Moving down with his lips kissing her soft skin. Then blowing hot air making her nipples really stiff. Then he could suck and flicked each of them with his tongue.

As he thought more about her naked body's his hand slipped down to his manhood which was starting to rise. He began to think about the copper mound and how playing with it was so much fun.

Then he thought about lying between her thighs and tasting her honey.

He shook his head, let go of his manhood and thought, *"Cold shower time or I will never get to the celebration."*

Shelbi meanwhile was in the shower soaping her body all over. As she washed the soap off, she looked down at her copper mound and smiled, "Yes, tonight my Prince will come."

. . . .

Several hours later as Shelbi turned the corner, she saw Brendenn walking towards her and she laughed out loud. Obviously, they had had the same thoughts at the same time.

"There's my wonderful Shelbi. I really like that blue dress. And those legs, I can't wait to run my fingers over the outsides and my lips on the insides of them," Brendenn thought.

As Shelbi met Brendenn and she stretched up on her toes in her red high-heeled and gave him a quick kiss on his warm lips.

Sabrinna came up beside her and reached up with her glass to toast. "To the best graduation and the greatest cadets!" And with that Shelbi clinked Brendenn's glass, Sabrinna's class, and then Sabrinna's partner's glass.

"Shelbi I would like to introduce my friend cadet Mathersonn," Sabrinna said glancing in the direction of her partner.

"It's my pleasure to meet anyone who can keep up with Sabrinna," Shelbi responded.

"Actually, she has to try to keep up with me," Mathersonn said with a smile on his face.

Shelbi wasn't sure exactly who he was. Was he just a friend or part of the protector group for Brendenn? It didn't take long to find out.

As the group walked towards the elevator to take them down from the convention center to the lobby a commotion was heard from an adjoining hallway. An obviously inebriated cadet stumbled out and started yelling in some strange dialect at Brendenn. Mathersonn move faster than Shelbi expected. He had the gentleman with his arm behind him and was frog marching him back down the hallway. Moments later he reappeared and simply smiled at Brendenn.

"Thank you for taking care of that inconvenience Mathersonn," Brendenn said.

As they reached the elevator a second couple join them smiling at the group. Sabrinna leaned over to Shelbi and said, "This is the second couple that will join us tonight. I would like to introduce cadet Johnsonn and cadet Allisonn his female friend."

Shelbi shook hands all around and began to understand that Brendenn would be well defended.

They cross the lobby and took the express elevator to the executive floors. When they got to the Royal suite Brendenn palmed the entrance and open the double doors so they could walk in.

Shelbi was somewhat taken back by the huge room they walked into. She looked across the two-story room. The entire wall was windows open to the outside showing a magnificent view of the city.

"This can hold about 80 people comfortably for any reception, party or whatever might be needed," Brendenn explained.

"My Uncle Samuelsonn was the architect of both this hotel and the convention center. He always builds a Royal suite in so there's a place for us to stay with a little extra security plus a great view of the city."

The two couples went off to the left set of stairs to the guest bedrooms. Brendenn grabbed Shelbi's hand and started up the stairs to the right. Again, a palm code was required to open the doors.

Shelbi smiled as she saw the huge room. Magnificent floor-to-ceiling windows showed a panoramic view of the city outside.

She walked over and stood looking out in wonderment.

Brendenn came up behind her and gave her a hug. Then he dropped to his knees and ran his fingers up the outside of her soft naked lags all the way to her lacy underwear thighs. It sent shivers up her skin as he did that and the heat started between her thighs. Her nipples also responded and felt stiff.

"I can't wait till she is naked and I can run my tongue over her soft skin. Then I can really enjoy making her shiver," He thought.

He ran his fingers slowly down the outside of her legs. She leaned forward and put her hands on the glass for support.

"The glassy you are leaning on is thermoplastic. It can take a large bomb and absorb the energy. It's also covered with a special reflecting material making so it one way. We can see out but no one can see in. It absorbs UV rays and allows just the natural sunlight to fall through."

He stood up and grabbed Shelbi's hand. "Let's continue the tour into the bathroom."

As they walked pass the bed into a room that could easily hold 10 people Shelbi looked at the pool size bathtub.

"Maybe I'll just do a few laps as a warm-up exercise in your tub. Does it really have to be that big?"

"Actually, it has a swimming lapping feature that you can turn on. It creates a jet stream so you can simply swim in place. Or you can just have some fun with your girlfriend as it caresses her body with the warm waves!"

Shelbi smiled, turned and her red high heels make clicking sounds as she walked across the ornate clay tiles out of the bathroom and onto the soft carpet of the bedroom.

Brendenn stood motionless watching her go as his eyes hungrily ran up her legs. *"I don't think my pants zipper can stand much more. I know my manhood has never been this aroused, this hard,"* he thought.

He ran out of the bathroom and before she could reach the bed, he placed his hands on her shoulders and spun her around facing him.

He bent down and lightly kissed her lips. As he started to rise up her hand grabbed the back of his neck and the urgency of her kiss stopped him. Their lips mashed together and her wet tongue began to explore his hot lips.

Her breasts crushed into his chest as her nipples tingle demanding she bare them so his hot lips could kiss them. A ripple of heat ran down her back as the lovers urge to feel his hard manhood crushed against her belly turned into a need. The need exploded into an urge almost like a mini climax.

Shelbi put her right hand on his chest and pushed him back one step, turn walked away. After taking two steps in her high heels, she turned around and commanded, "Brendenn stay."

A smile crossed his handsome face. "That will cost you Shelbi."

"I'm counting on it."

She walked around the end of the bed and over to a chair and turned to face him. She unzipped the back of her blue dress and slipped it off her shoulders. Dropping it to the floor she stepped out of it and carefully folded it over the back of the chair.

Standing still for a moment Brendenn admired her frilly bra, lacy pants and red shoes combine with her fiery red hair and wonderful alabaster skin silhouetted by the city light coming through the window.

Her nipples were hard against the bra fabric demanding to be freed. She slowly took the straps off her shoulders then reach behind her and undid the clasp. Folding it on the chair she added her panties then she turned and walked towards Brendenn.

His eyes hungrily roamed up her bare legs to her blue frilly briefs. Then on up to the magnificent swaying breasts as she walked towards him. At the same time, he was busy unbuttoning his shirt and before she reached him, he turned around and draped it over the back of the chair.

She hugged her naked breasts against his bare abdomen. Pushing her thighs against his hardness still trapped in his pants she ran her fingers down his bare back.

Shelbi step back and stepped out of her red high heels and place them at the end of the bed.

She then began to undo his belt, and pulled it out of his pant loop's. As she did that his hands went to the top and undid the pants. Then he stepped out of them and folded them over the chair.

She gazed at his dark black silky briefs and the ridge his manhood was forcing against the front of them.

He swept her off her feet and kneeling on the edge of the bed carefully later down with her head on the pillow. Stepping back to slipped off the boxers he dropped them on the other chair.

As he lay down beside her, she could feel his hot rigid manhood pulsing against her warm thigh. The pulsing shot across her leg and started a matching rhythm in her clitoris.

His lips began kissing her neck and traveled down across her breast to circle her erect nipples. Slowly his tongue began rotating around the pebbled flush of her right nipple. Meanwhile his thumb and forefinger tweaked her left nipple.

His hand then roamed down across her belly leaving a trail of sensation. As it came to her copper mound the fingers stop their travels and rested creating more heat. Her sensitive nub was begging for attention and created a slight shudder as his fingers denied its need.

Her arm fell down beside her body and came in contact with his rigid member. Slowly she began to stroke it.

He rolled away from her for a moment and came back quickly popping a magic membrane on the tip of his manhood. It slid down his erection covering it in a fine film.

His lips returned to her tented right nipple. He kissed her lightly and then moved across to kiss the pert nipple on her left breast.

Slowly he kisses his way down her warm stomach stopping at her red copper mound.

As he did this, she slowly ran her fingers over his back applying more pressure with her nails as her tension rose. She could feel the trail of pebbled bumps they were left behind her fingers. She knew he was enjoying this as the sensation was rolling over his body.

Brendenn thought, *"If she keeps up caressing my back like that it won't be able to focus on my journey to her sweet nectar."*

He moved his lips over her swollen nub and gently began to caress it with his tongue. At the same time his finger moved up and down her glistening lips feeling the honey coated surface.

Shelbi reached down and intertwined her fingers in the back of his neck. She was urging him to help her reach the climax she knew was coming. The energy was building she just needed a little more to push her over the edge.

He moved his mouth off her bud and began trailing his warm tongue up and down the swollen lips of her vagina. As he felt her thighs tensing against his cheek he moved back up to her swollen clitoris and began to torture it.

Shelbi could stand no more and pushed him undo his back. She quickly straddled him and reached between her hot thighs to grab his magic member rod. She stroked it up-and-down her slippery lips.

As Brendenn tried to stop her, she rose up slightly teasing him with a smile.

Slowly she slid down feeling him fill her hot channel with a pulsating thrill. When he had completely filled her, she stopped for a moment. Brendenn had cupped her breasts and his thumbs were working on her sensitive nipples stroking them back and forth.

She locked both her feet over his thighs and began the rhythmic dance sliding her hot throbbing vagina lips up-and-down his pulsating member.

He placed his hands on her hips and felt her breasts slide up and down his chest rubbing across his nipples creating a great warmth and sensation in his chest.

His hands began to rome up-and-down her back caressing the soft skin. Shelbi now had more sensations than she could almost handle. His fingers sent shivers up-and-down her back. Her nipples rubbing his chest sending shocks down between her thighs. In the continuing movement of him sliding in and out of her vagina was building her towards a wonderful climax.

Suddenly, he rolled her over on her back and took up the tempo of plunging in and out of her warmth. She used one hand on her breast to play with her nipple and the other hand on his chest caressing his nipple.

He leaned down and kissed her, and she opened her lips to welcome his sensual tongue.

That their tongues dancing together in the rhythm of him between her thighs her climax came as her whole body shuddered and shook with him deep insider. His timing matched her moments later with the powerful climax gushing the Royal seed into the magic member.

She rolled to her side and quickly slid him back between her thighs. She wasn't ready to let go of this sensation yet. As he cuddled her into his hot naked body, she felt his breath returning to normal.

"My Shelbi that really was a royal moment."

"Only the first one for tonight my Brendenn."

Shelbi rested for moment thinking about what a tremendous graduation this had been so far. With those fleeting thoughts she reached up and kissed him to start their next sensual round.

Rebel Alien Passion
The Next Shelbi MacPhadden Passion Adventure!

Chapter 1: Air Cruiser Danger and Chance Meeting

Shelbi's dark blue R398 air cruiser suddenly turns right and started to quickly descend into a long dark alley. She fought with the controls but could not stop the downward movement as it hit hard on the dusty grey tarmac.

She knew this could be trouble. This was not the best place in town to be. She tried caming the tech center to send a repair cruiser. All she got was the snake hiss of static.

Shelbi pressed the red emergency security locator and watched with some satisfaction as the beam went out and was acknowledged. "Help will arrive in 12 minutes." The recorded voice claimed.

She opened the door and exited the damaged vehicle taking her gun out of her leather holster. Having just comes from headquarters gathering the files about her new mission to capture the rebel leader she was glad she had gone armed.

Off to the left several individuals emerged out of the dark doorway. As they walk towards her, she realized there were five of them and one of her.

Still, if necessary and this got messy she could disarm several of them.

On the second-floor balcony of a grey building nearby, a large individual had watched her land cruiser raise dust as it slammed into the dark alley road.

"What stupid person would fly in here?" He thought.

"Don't get out of the car," The thought transferred across his mind. He almost yelled out loud but was certain the person wouldn't hear him with the distance between them.

Sure enough, she emerged from her car. He was immediately surprised by the flaming red hair. He had known many women that had black, brown or even blonde hair, but the red hair immediately created interest.

He noted her military stance as she appeared to unholster a weapon.

Then to his dismay he saw the five characters emerge from the building. He knew exactly what had happened. They had hacked into her air cruiser and pulled into the alley. This was going to be trouble, big trouble.

Reacting not thinking, he quickly strode inside, across the room, out into the dark hallway and to the end stairwell. Taking the stairs two at a time he emerged out the side door at the same time the five large grubby individuals started to circle the car.

"Am I in my talking to the leader?" Shelbi stated to the individual standing in front of her.

"Yes. Do you have some trouble with your cruiser?" He sneered.

"Yes, for some reason it's landed here. Technology must be dysfunctional. I've called for an emergency repair unit."

"You called for an ER unit? Perhaps we can help you."

"No that's fine I'll wait for the ER unit." She was careful not to mention that it was a security ER unit that would be arriving to help her.

Two of them were now standing beside Shelbi.

"I like to ask you politely to step away," she said looking side to side at the scruffy individuals.

They laughed out loud and began to push up against her.

She turned and swung her right knee into the creature standing beside her dropping him to the ground with a swift crotch kick.

As she whirled back the four began to grab and push her.

Shelbi thought, *Things were definitely out of control.*

A large dark-haired man swept around the back of the car knocking two men out of the way.

"Honey it's so good to see you," he said as he rushed up to Shelbi and gathered her in his arms and gave her a big kiss on her open mouth.

He pulled his head away and looked at her face as the thought raced through his mind that he felt something kissing her he hadn't felt for a long time.

Shelbi had not reacted to him rushing up because she'd been so surprised. But as he kissed her, she felt the warmth flow down to her tender parts. *"That was really unusual,"* She thought.

The big man swung around and stuck out his hand towards the leader.

"Howdy my name's Bo Pinky. I wanna thank you for protecting my lady. It's not such a great area."

Turning to Shelbi he pulled her into his chest, "Are you are OK honey?"

"My name's Jackson. Where did you come from?" the leader asked.

"Your name's Jackson who?"

"Just Jackson"

"Well Just Jackson I live in the building over there."

"Bo Pinky, why that name? Nobody lives in that building it's empty?"

"Oh, Bo Pinky's my nickname from when I was in the Marines. I could kill a man with just my pinky. I did it enough times the name stuck. Ya, I now live in the building. Granite Security was hired to protect the building. I was hire today to work it. And I get to live in any suite I want." A goofy grin crossed his jutting jaw as he said the last sentence.

"You work for Granite Security and they're taking over the building?"

"Yes. And I guess my honeys here to help me pick out the suite I want to live in. Thanks again for taking care of her."

"Not so fast Bo. I run this neighbourhood. I'm not sure were finished here."

Bo looked at him and just for a moment the leader thought he saw a flash in Bo's eyes. Maybe he was not the country bumkin after all.

Bo smiled and said, "Then I'm goanna ask you to grant me a favour. You and your friends have had some fun but let's leave my honey alone. You see she's my responsibility and I don't want to lose my job because I have had another, ah, incident as the Marines used to call it."

"Bo, I'm going to grant you that favour. If we should ever meet again, I expect you to remember it. My name's Jason Ainge and where the Steel Murd group. You owe me a favour."

The leader made a signal with his hand and the five gang members turned and vanished into the dark ally.

Shelbi turned to the man and whispered n his ear. "OK we both know you are not Bo Pinky. What is your real name marine?"

The large man turned towards her. Slowly putting out his hand, "Hello my name's Nicholson Maglow. I hope you're okay?"

"Thank you, Nicholson Maglow. That could have gotten very messy and somehow, I think with five of them and one of me I would might not have won so easily. I'm in your debt."

"If we ever meet again, I may take you up on that. Have you called for assistance or help?"

"Yes, I push the ER beam that they should be here in the next 3 minutes."

"That's wonderful. I'll stay with you till they arrived. This is not a good part of town to be stranded. I suspect those gang people jammed your technology and that's why you landed here. This R398 air cruiser is one of the top of the line and they would've loved to strip it."

"Yes, how did you know?"

"Just a lucky guess?"

Nickleson took Shelbi's hand and started to walk around the back of the car. She pulled him to a stop and reached up and gave him a warm kiss. *"Funny that sent that warm rush again,"* she thought.

He had felt the warmth of her kiss, a warmth he hadn't felt for some time. "We really need to get off the street. They granted us a favour this time but they're not the only pack in the area," he said.

As they walked toward the building he continued. "I would suggest you don't come back here. This is not a good part of town to be stranded in. Out of curiosity was your phone jammed when you tried it?"

"Yes, it was. But fortunately, the cruiser has an emergency call button that wasn't jammed."

As the flash of the emergency rescue cruiser came closer Nickleson smiled at her. "I take my leave now I don't really want to be around when they're here. I hope you have a better day."

He bent down and gave her alight kiss. Her hand swept up behind his head and pressed is muscular neck. She held the kiss for several sweet seconds.

"Sorry, I don't know why I did that. I don't even know you," Shelbi blurted.

Shelbi watched him disappear and wondered who he really was.

The rescue cruiser landed and then Shelbi noticed there were two other security cruisers behind them. Very quickly a number of armed security people were deployed around the vehicle.

A tall well-built man strode up to Shelbi and she recognized him as Sergeant Taylor in charge of the company security.

"I think you've fallen into the category where they tried to seize the vehicle. They probably jam the technology and guided you down. It's a good thing we have the ER button installed they haven't figured out how to jam that yet. I trust you are, OK? Do you need medical support?" As he finished his speech Shelbi could see that he was clearly upset about this turn of events.

"Sargent not to worry."

She walked over to one of the waiting vehicles and slid into the passenger side. Shelbi did not need medical support. She hadn't felt nervous or upset. She had merely been focused on the events as they unravelled and was thinking how to defend yourself.

As she sat alone in the vehicle, and thought back to how should become a warrior Princess Elite cadet.

As a young lady growing up, she really enjoyed computer games and technology. At a very young age she got involved with team sports along with other boys and girls. Her parents recognizing her ambition and had created a custom fit fighting suit for her when she was 13. As she grew into it with curvy hips and larger breasts, they had it redesigned to fit.

She had loved the strategy and execution of wargames. And she had always wanted to be involved with the warrior Princess Elite Academy.

She applied after her nineteenth birthday and was pleasantly surprised when she was accepted with her very first application. Since then, she was sophisticatedly trained to adapt, survive and kill in both military combat scenarios and to build inter-world uniting relationships.

Then her mind drifted to the large man. She had been surprised by his dark brown hair and piercing grey eyes. His short sleeve T-shirt showed off his amazing biceps. Yet when he reached out to shake her hand it was a gentle touch. And those kisses.

"Not the time to think about sex Shelbi," She thought to herself. However, he was an amazingly well-built man. And she had been eleven weeks without aerobic sex or in fact any kind of sex that didn't involve just herself.

Arriving back at her suite she found a new R398 blue air cruiser parked in her high security parking space.

She went into her bedroom and stripped off her clothes.

Standing in the dark dank alley some of the dust that had swirled around when the rescue cruisers landed had gotten into her hair, her teeth and layered her skin. She really needed a nice hot shower.

As she grabbed the soap and began to lather her body she thought back to Nicholson. How nice it would be to have him soaping her body.

She began to rub the soap over her breasts creating a slippery surface. The more she kneaded them the perkier her nipples got. The urgency in their tenseness set her using her thumbs to gently caressed each warm tip. That sent the warmth down her stomach to her thighs.

"I think it's pleasure time. After what I just went through, I've earned it. But Nicholson being here would have been better," she said.

She began to soap her stomach with her right hand and her fingers travelled up and down causing the skin to pebble. As she ran the soap over her copper mound and between her thighs, she could feel her vagina lips starting to tingle.

She lightly soaped them and then paid attention to her fingers rubbing the soap off in the hot water.

The warmth of her bud at the top of her lower lips was amazing. The tingling she felt was just begging to be caressed. As her fingers slid up and down her vagina lips, they became silky with her own essence. She began to used her thumb back and forth on her sensitive clitoris.

Her other hand kneaded her breasts and flicked her nipples creating more heat and sensual feelings across them.

She dropped the soap and used her fingers and a rhythm that sped up faster and faster. She could feel her climax building as she continued to rub the erect bud. Slowly she pushed a finger inside and moved it back and forth in her vagina.

As the tension rose to became more urgent, she flicked her clitoris back and forth in a climax building rhythm. Two fingers were now rhythmically inserting inside her vagina and sliding back out again. The rhythm of the two hands continued until that moment when the climax overtook her, leaving her long legs trembling and her ample breasts shaking.

She paused as the hot water continue to pour over her body and enjoyed the physical satisfaction of pleasuring oneself.

She decided right there and then she'd have to try and find out more about this Nicholson Maglow person. Little did she know that Nicholson would become an important part of her life as a target she was to capture or kill or love.

To Be Continued . . . .

Look for this next Shelbi MacPhadden, Warrior Princes Elite adventure, **Rebel Alien Passion** *book soon.*

The Shelbi MacPhadden Adventures.

Free for Every One
Fulfilled Alien Passion
Shelbi MacPhadden Adventure 1
Everyone can use this Amazon link for a free copy.
https://www.amazon.com/gp/product/B08P8M89N
9

For FREE! *Kindle Unlimited Readers can read the following Shelbi MacPhadden adventures for fun, adventure and personal pleasure.*

Desert Alien Passion
Shelbi MacPhadden Adventure 2
You can purchase your personal e-book copy or print copy on amazon by clicking here:
 https://www.amazon.com/dp/B07HL1SZTV

Electric Alien Passion
Shelbi MacPhadden Adventure 3
You can purchase your personal e-book copy or print copy on amazon by clicking here:
https://www.amazon.com/dp/B07KNP16B2

Warrior Alien Passion
Shelbi MacPhadden Adventure 4

 You can purchase your personal e-book copy or print copy on amazon by clicking here:
https://www.amazon.com/dp/B083BY57MG
Here is to your personal excitement and passion!

About Sharon Barrington

Sharon Barrington started writing for fun and wanted to share it. Her books are for you, if you enjoy science fiction adventure on distant planets, combined with sexy feel, good erotica passion with strong alien naked men.

For other Shelbi MacPhadden adventures or to be notified when new releases come out please go to her Amazon author page or sign up for her book flashes at authorsharonbarrington@live.com

Sharon really thanks all those who leave reviews - they really help share with others Shelbi's wonderful erotic alien passion adventures.

Enjoy your own personal passion!

Sharon Barrington